power

THE
keatyn
CHRONICLES
power

JILLIAN DODD

Published by Swoonworthy Books, an imprint of Jillian Dodd, Inc.
www.jilliandodd.net

Jillian Dodd, The Keatyn Chronicles, Spy Girl, and Kitty Valentine are registered trademarks of Jillian Dodd, Inc.

ISBN: 978-1-953071-58-3

Books by Jillian Dodd

London Prep
The Exchange
The Boys' Club
The Kiss
The Key
The Party

The Keatyn Chronicles®
Stalk Me
Kiss Me
Date Me
Love Me
Adore Me
Hate Me
Get Me
Fame
Power
Money
Sex
Love
A Very Keatyn Christmas
Keatyn Unscripted
Aiden

That Boy
That Boy
That Wedding
That Baby
That Love

That Ring
That Summer
That Promise

Kitty Valentine

Kitty Valentine dates a Billionaire
Kitty Valentine dates a Doctor
Kitty Valentine dates a Rockstar
Kitty Valentine dates a Fireman
Kitty Valentine dates an Actor
Kitty Valentine dates the Best Man
Kitty Valentine dates a Cowboy
Kitty Valentine dates a Hockey Player
Kitty Valentine dates Santa

Crawford Brothers

Vegas Love
Broken Love
Fake Love

Spy Girl®

The Prince
The Eagle
The Society
The Valiant
The Dauntless
The Phoenix
The Echelon

Girl off the Grid

Tuesday, October 7th

VANESSA'S ESTATE, GUEST HOUSE — HOLMBY HILLS
ARIELA

"COLLIN! STOP IT!" I yell, pulling away from his unwanted kiss.

He grabs my arms tightly, digging his fingers in. "You're my wife. You need to come with me."

"How did you get in here?" I ask, wondering how he got through the gate.

"I told the phone company we were in California on vacation and you misplaced your phone. They gave me the GPS coordinates. The gate was open. You told your parents you were staying in a friend's guest house. And here I am."

I shove the divorce papers toward him. "Take these. It's time you face the facts. We're getting a divorce. We're not getting back together, and I'm *not* coming home!"

He leans closer to me, like he's going to kiss me again, but instead he whispers, "But, pumpkin, you got up in front of 478 people and promised '*Til death do us part.*"

"And you promised to be faithful. You broke our vows, Collin, not me."

"I told you I'd stop seeing her."

"No, you told me you already had, but we both know you lied about it. You need to leave, now!" I shout.

"I'm not leaving without you!"

"Yes, you are," a voice says.

Collin spins around to find Chad, Vanessa's buff, massage-giving pool boy standing behind him. Chad's arms are crossed in front of his chest, his muscles bulging from beneath a tight white T-shirt.

"Who the fuck do you think you are?" Collin asks haughtily. "I'm her *husband*."

"Who she is divorcing. I will escort you out now or have you arrested for trespassing. Your choice."

Collin studies Chad closely and I know which option he will choose. Although he tries to act tough, he's not a fighter. He's too soft.

"This isn't over, Ariela," he says to me, as he allows Chad to lead him away.

Collin stares at me the whole time Chad is dragging him down the stone path. That's when I notice a pink bouquet lying on the ground.

Riley!

I run toward the house so fast that I pass Chad and Collin, looking for him. When I get to the front of the house, I see a single pink petal lying on the driveway. I pick it up and stare at it.

As Collin walks by me, he knocks it out of my hand. "I'm going to make your life miserable, baby. That's a promise."

"You don't know *how* to keep promises, *baby*," I sass back before he screeches out of the driveway.

I turn to Chad. "Was Riley here?"

"I haven't seen him."

I rush back to the guest house, stopping to pick up the beautiful bouquet of pink peonies. When we first dated, I told Collin they were my favorite flower, but he always insisted that red roses were better. When we dated later in college, he asked me again. This time I lied, telling him I loved red roses. I would have died if he ever bought me anything pink. Pink was something I shared with Riley. When Riley asked me to be his girlfriend, he gave me a pink rhinestone Hello Kitty ring. On our one-year anniversary, he filled my dorm room with an assortment of pink flowers. The peonies were my favorite and Riley said they would forever be our flower. Part of me can't believe he remembers. But our love left such an imprint on our souls that neither of us could ever forget.

I set the bouquet down on the kitchen counter while I grab my phone and call him.

It goes straight to voicemail.

Could Riley have seen me with Collin? Is that why he dropped the flowers and left?

I call again and get no answer, so I decide to text him.

Me: Hey, are we still on for tonight?

When he doesn't reply, I send another.

Me: I found the flowers, Riley. Please call me.

My hands shake as I fill a vase with water for the peonies. I set the gorgeous arrangement on the sofa table then go up to the main house, finding Vanessa in the kitchen.

"I heard your ex was here," she says as she pours me a drink. "You need this?"

I gratefully take the drink.

"You're shaking," she says. "What happened?"

"I'm not even sure," I say, taking a gulp. "I opened the door happily expecting Riley but found Collin standing there instead."

"What did he say?"

"That he wants me to come home. That he'll stop cheating. When I said no, he grabbed me and kissed me. And now I'm freaking out because I'm afraid Riley might have seen."

"What makes you think that? Dawson just texted me to cancel our dinner plans. Something about a last minute business trip with his brother."

"That's weird." I double-check my phone. "He didn't call or text me. Did Dawson say where they're going?"

"Nope. Just that he had to go straight to the airport."

"Weird."

"What makes you think Riley was here? Because I'm pretty sure if Riley saw you kissing someone, he would have been pissed and let you know it."

"I found a bouquet of pink peonies on the ground. Peonies are our flower. Could you call Dawson and ask him if Riley was here?" I plead.

"Sure, I can." She puts her phone up to her ear. "Hmm. Straight to voicemail. But, you know, there is another way we can find out if he was here."

"How?"

She grabs a remote and turns on the TV. "What time were you expecting him?"

"Six."

She clicks a few buttons. "This house has video security." She rewinds back to 5:55. "Well, that's a problem," she says as we watch Riley drive through the gate. My heart starts beating wildly when I see that he still has his green Viper. I remember one of our first dates, so vividly.

"God, you're beautiful," Riley says, making me blush when he greets me with a kiss outside my dorm.

I look at the ground, embarrassed. I'm not used to those kind of compliments.

He puts his hand under my chin and gently raises it so that I have to look in his eyes. "I'm going to tell you that every day until you believe it. To me, you're the most beautiful girl in the world." He gives me a cute grin. "I have a surprise for you tonight."

"What kind of surprise?" I ask.

"I'm going to let you drive my car."

"Really?" I say in shock. "I overheard you tell Dallas that you'd never let some girl drive it."

"You're not just some *girl," he says, melting my heart. "Do you know how to drive a stick?"*

"No."

"Then it's about time you learn."

"I can't believe the gate was just open like that!" Vanessa yells, snapping me back to the present. "Bernard! Get in here. Why was the gate open?"

"I knew Mr. Johnson was expected and being proactive."

"You know that's not how we do things."

"Yes, Ms. Flanning, I apologize. It will not happen again."

"That explains how Collin got in," I mutter, but then I watch Riley. "See, he's getting out of the car and he has the bouquet. Are there cameras in the back yard too?"

"No, just the gate, the front door, and the perimeter outside the gate."

I'm holding my breath waiting for Riley to come back on screen, hoping he's on his phone with some emergency.

There's a flash of his face on the screen. "Pause that!"

"He's pissed," Vanessa says.

"Shit. He must have seen Collin."

"Or maybe he got a phone call and was mad he had to leave."

"Is it normal for him to take off on a moment's notice for business?"

"Actually, it is. Captive is currently filming four different movies. Something could've gone wrong on a set—a director threatening to quit, one of the big stars getting into trouble. It doesn't happen often but it does happen."

"So why didn't he bring me the flowers, give me a kiss, and tell me he had to leave?"

"It could be because he saw Collin, but I highly doubt it. If he would have seen, Riley would have confronted you. I think he got a call, was pissed he had to leave, dropped the flowers, and left. I'm sure he'll text you later. He's probably on the phone dealing with it and can't call. Just leave him a message and tell him I told you about the trip."

"Okay."

"What's more important, though, is dealing with your ex. Chad said he escorted him out. Why was he even here? How did he find you?"

"We have that thing where you can find your lost phone. He tracked it here."

"Why did he come?"

"To give me back the divorce papers. He wanted me to

go home with him. When I said no, he threatened to contest the divorce forever."

"He can't contest it forever, but he can make your life miserable during what can be a long, drawn-out process. That I know. My divorce took two years to get finalized."

"I don't want it to take that long."

"Then it's time to play hardball, Ariela."

"I'm not good at that."

"Then I can't help you."

"It's not that I don't want to, it's just . . ."

"Ariela, you have to decide what you can live with. Can you put your life on hold for a couple years while you wait to get a divorce? Can you live with the emotional devastation it will cause you? Can you listen to his lame excuses for why he's an asshole and wants you back?"

"When I decided to come here, something inside me sort of snapped. I know this is the right decision for me. I've just got to get back some of my—"

"Confidence. You're a beautiful, talented woman, Ariela, and I get it. My relationship with Bam stripped my confidence and my dignity. Sometimes, though, you have to hit rock bottom before you realize that you need to make a change."

"I'm at the bottom now. I'm willing to do whatever it takes. I already threatened to tell my dad about the affair, but my dad will be neither shocked nor appalled that he's unfaithful. If anything, he'll probably sympathize with him."

"You'll have to use the photos then," Vanessa states. "But here's a question. If Collin has a lot of loyal clients, couldn't he take them all to another firm if your dad decided to take your side?"

"Not really. My dad spoon-feeds him business. He

doesn't really work that hard."

"So if we want to hurt him, we take away his clients. If his clients start leaving him, would that affect your dad?"

"Yes, my dad gets a cut from everyone's sales. That's why he gives Collin so many customers, because they are still ultimately his."

"Is it normal for someone so young to make partner?"

"Not at all."

"So the other reps at the firm probably resent him?"

"Yeah, they see how easy he has it."

"You mentioned that he wants kids, so he'll look stable. He wanted you to go on a weekend event for the same reason."

"Appearances are important to him. The perfect marriage. Perfect house. Lots of luxury items to make him appear more successful than he is."

"Hmm," Vanessa says, tapping a perfectly manicured nail on the table. I look down at my own nails. I've nervously scraped off most of the polish.

"The holiday season is coming up," she says.

"Yeah?"

"Does your husband send out holiday cards?"

"Actually, he sends out Thanksgiving cards since his clients celebrate different holidays and he doesn't want to offend anyone."

"Maybe he should send out one of those cute photo cards this year." She grins. "Or, better yet, a photo collage."

"Of him and his secretary? Do you think his clients will be like my dad and not care?"

"Maybe, but I bet in most households the wives open the mail."

"If the wives were offended, that could ruin him."

"Only if you actually sent it. I'm not saying you should. I'm just saying you just have to convince him that you will."

"I'd need his client list," I say, thinking it through.

"Can you get that?"

I smile to myself. "I think I can. In fact, I'm going to call my dad, right now, before Collin talks to him." I take a cleansing breath. "Here goes nothing."

My dad answers with, "I assume you're calling to tell me that you and Collin are back together. I want to go on record that I deserve all the credit. I told him he needed to just go out there and get you."

"Collin was here, Dad. We got into a fight and he left. But after he left, I had a change of heart and decided to come back home. I apologize for the disrespectful way in which I spoke to you the other day. I know that you and Mom were able to work past it, so I'm hoping Collin and I will be able to follow your shining example."

"That's my girl."

"Oh, and Dad, I was thinking of a way I could make it up to Collin. You know how Mom's been telling me that I should put my event planning skills to good use as a volunteer? Well, I want to do something special for Collin. I thought instead of his usual Thanksgiving cards, I'd send out party invitations instead. I want to design an amazing event for his clients to attend. Do you think he'd like that?"

"Darling, I think he'd love that. I'm so proud of you."

"Don't tell him, please. I want it to be a surprise."

"Mum's the word."

"Thanks, Dad. That means a lot to me. Will you help me?"

"Of course. Anything you need."

"Well, to send out invitations, I'd need a list of his

clients' home addresses. I'd hate to ask his secretary. I'm afraid she might tell him and ruin the surprise."

"She is a bit of a gossip. Tell you what, I'll download the list myself and email it directly to you. I've got my laptop here at home. Give me a few minutes."

"Oh, thank you, Dad. You have no idea how much this means to me."

"Glad to help. Call your mother and make dinner plans soon."

"Thanks, I will."

When I hang up, Vanessa says, "Oh, you're good."

"I feel guilty lying to my dad."

"He and your mother have been lying to you for years about their relationship."

"Good point," I say, as my phone dings. "I just got the email from my dad. Now what?"

"Now, we play hardball. Leave Collin a message, apologizing, and asking him to call you."

PENTHOUSE SUITE – VEGAS
RILEY

I'M LYING ON a circular bed on a raised platform with Jennifer, passing her a joint, and watching Dawson slide down the fireman's pole from the second floor.

"This is like some crazy fantasy of mine," she says, as much to herself as to me. She was hitting the champagne pretty hard on the flight here. Hell, we all were. "Me and three hot guys alone in a freaking outrageous Vegas suite."

"What do the guys do in this fantasy?" I ask, as Knox screams his way down the pole.

"Their hands are all over me. They all think I'm beautiful."

"So, you up for that tonight?"

She sighs. "Sadly, no. I'd never be able to look any of you in the eye again. I'm pretty sure my three guys are strangers who I'd never have to see again. Like *ever*. Would you do that, Riley? Three guys, one girl?" She turns and looks at me. "Or have you already?"

"I'd prefer the three girls to one guy fantasy."

"Have you ever done that?"

I smile. "Maybe."

"It's a yes or no question."

"Depends on what you're referring to. Three in the same night or three at the same time?"

"Same time."

"No. Only two."

"I would never do that with you, Riley. Just for the record."

"Why not?"

"Because even after your stupidity at the vineyard, I still respect you."

"We'd have fun, I promise."

"No."

"I don't mean you, me, and Knox. I mean just the two of us. So you and Knox fucked. Big deal. I don't care. We can still have fun."

"Which is the problem, Riley. You *should* care. So what happened with Ariela? Knox said the other day you were on cloud nine." She looks around. "And now we're nearing the pits of hell."

"I went to pick her up and she was kissing her husband."

"Then fuck her."

"Yeah, fuck her."

"It's her loss. It really is." She grabs my arm. "Oh, Riley, I think I drank too much. The bed is spinning."

"It *is* spinning."

"Did you drink too much too?"

"No, I mean the bed *actually* rotates."

She sits up. "Oh, thank god. I'm not as drunk as I thought."

"Let's drink to that."

We run to the bar, pour shots of something, making extras for Knox and Dawson.

"Here's to . . . Uh, October?" Knox salutes.

"No wait! I know," Jennifer yells, sloshing her shot. "It's not October! It's *Cock*tober! So, here's to *Cock*tober. Hoping the use of yours is, um, plentiful and I get plenty for myself."

We all down our shots and then she says, "Uh, that sounded slutty. I didn't mean I want all your cocks."

Knox lays a big kiss on her lips. "Naw, sugar, you only want mine."

After she kisses him, she pulls us all on the bed with her. "Let's take one more spin on the bed!"

Knox pops up when his phone rings.

Dawson pips me on the forehead, taunting me like he did when we were kids. But Jennifer leans on her side and faces me. "I'm glad you're not mad at me, Riley."

"You're too cute to stay mad at," I tell her.

KNOX ENDS HIS call. "Our guy's here!" He gives me a wink then turns to Jennifer. "So, the plan is we go to some dance clubs and later we'll invite some cool people back here to party."

"What, no strip clubs?" Jennifer asks, exactly as he'd hoped.

"Oh, sugar, I wasn't sure how you felt about strip clubs. A lot of girls aren't confident enough to go to them."

"I've never been to a Vegas strip club. It sounds like an adventure. I say we do that!"

"Well, if you insist," Knox replies.

"I insist," she says. "And what else should we do? I know! We'll go dancing, get thrown out of a club, maybe get arrested, get married." She bounces in place next to Knox. "Wouldn't that be an adventure? Wanna get wasted and get married?"

Knox pulls her into a hug. "That's the thing about Vegas. No planning. You just go with the flow." He pats her back while he looks at me and Dawson and mouths, *No fucking way!*

As we leave the suite, I wrap my arm around my brother's neck. "Tonight's gonna be a good night."

AND IT WAS . . . Until we ended up in jail.

"Riley Johnson, you can make your call now," the policeman says, opening the cell door.

I look down at myself, wondering what the fuck I'm wearing.

The night is kind of a blur but I do remember running down the hotel hallway naked, chasing a hooker who I thought stole my wallet. Then Jennifer started stripping and invited everyone to participate in *the naked party parade.*

I stare at the phone for a second, knowing who I need to call but dreading it.

Dallas is the only one who can make this mess go away.

For all of us.

"Riley?" he answers groggily. It's five in the morning and Dallas is not an early riser. "Tell me you're not in jail."

"I'm in jail."

"Fuck. I was joking. Where? What happened?"

"Vegas. Party. Drunk. Naked."

"You and Ariela went to Vegas?"

"No. When I went to pick her up, she was kissing her husband."

"Oh, shit."

"Exactly. So I decided to go to Vegas for the night with Knox and Dawson."

"Can't one of them bail you out—wait, did they get arrested?"

"Yeah," I admit, hanging my head. "Jennifer too."

"I'll be there as soon as I can."

"Thanks, man."

"Riley, we need to talk. Seriously."

"Yeah, I know. I fucked up bad this time."

Wednesday, October 8th

KEATYN & AIDEN'S BEACH HOUSE — MALIBU
KEATYN

MY CELL PHONE wakes me. I see that Dallas is calling and quickly answer.

"We have a problem," he says.

"What's wrong?!" I exclaim, waking Aiden up. "Is RiAnne okay?"

"She just had a contraction and you remember how fast the last baby came. We're on our way to the hospital."

"Do you need me to do something? Come watch the kids?"

He takes a deep breath. "Riley called me just before all hell broke loose at my house. He, Knox, Dawson, and our little angel, Jennifer, were arrested in Vegas. I'm supposed to bail them out, but now I can't."

"Why are they in Vegas? I thought Riley had a date with Ariela?"

"She was kissing someone, presumably her husband, when he got there."

"Oh, man. Poor Riley."

"We need to get Ariela out of here. She's fucking with his life. And when she fucks with his life, she's fucking with ours too. With our company. Can you imagine the press if this gets out?"

"Shit. I'll call Vanessa and see what she can do. You go to the hospital and take care of your wife. I'll go to Vegas."

"Thanks, call me when you know more."

"You do the same. Tell RiAnne I said I'm sending her good vibes for a quick, painless, and healthy delivery."

"Will do."

I hang up, drop my phone on the bed, and plop back on my pillow.

"What's going on?" Aiden asks.

"RiAnne is in labor. Riley is in jail."

"In Vegas?"

"Yes, I need to go bail them out."

He slides his hand down my arm. "Surely, you can just wire the money."

"That isn't really the point, Aiden. It's not just Riley. It's Dawson, Knox, and Jennifer. I don't know what all went down, but we need to pray there aren't any pictures."

"You aren't going anywhere. What you need to do is go back to sleep. I'll take care of bailing them out."

"I can't go back to sleep, Aiden. This is all my fault."

He pulls me into his arms and hugs me. "It's not your fault."

"Yes, it is! I'm the one who saw Ariela and invited her to dinner. Riley was so excited to take her out. He was talking to Dallas about how they had made love the night before. How he'd never be able to sleep with anyone else. That she ruined him. Dallas called it true love's fuck. It was so beautiful that it made me cry."

Aiden kisses my nose and puts his hand across my stomach. "Pregnancy has your hormones crazy right now."

"That may be true, but I started this whole mess. I'm pissed at Riley for getting arrested, but I also feel responsible. And although I want to just go hug him, I'm also worried that his arrest could have a negative effect on our business. What if the board gets wind of it?"

"Why don't you have some breakfast then meet Vanessa at the office? She can help you sort it all out. Do some damage control, if need be. Boots, I don't want you getting stressed about this." He bends down and kisses my belly. "It's not good for you or our baby."

I reach for one of the gingersnap cookies Grandma made me, grab it out of the plastic bag on my nightstand, and shove it in my mouth. "Breakfast is over. Go, please. Now. Or *I'm* going."

He gives me one more kiss and gets out of bed.

The second he leaves the bedroom, I call Vanessa and Tyler and ask them to meet me at the office as soon as possible.

VANESSA'S ESTATE – HOLMBY HILLS
VANESSA

I'M PULLED OUT of a hot dream, where Dawson and I are having sex on the ridiculously expensive gold inlaid saddle that Bam bought me, by my ringing phone.

I rub my eyes, pick up the phone, and answer a call from Keatyn.

"I was having a really hot dream. This better be good," I tease her.

"Who were you with this time?" she asks. I'm always telling her about my random hot dreams. She's even turned a few of them into scenes in her movie scripts.

"Dawson."

"Oh—um, so the reason I'm calling is because I need your help. Like, right now."

I quickly sit up and grab a pen and notepad off my nightstand. "What's going on?"

"Riley, Knox, Jennifer, and Dawson went to Vegas last night. It was wild. I expect we'll need some damage control on this. Knox and Jennifer are too famous for someone not to have noticed them. And you know how the tabloids scour the arrest records."

"Who got arrested?!"

"All of them."

"Do you know what they did? The circumstances behind the arrest?" I ask.

"I'm not sure," she says. "Dallas was going to take care of bailing them out. But then RiAnne started having contractions, so he had to take her to the hospital."

"Oh, I'm so excited to find out what they have! I think it's a boy. She seemed to be carrying the baby low."

"I think it's a boy too. We'll find out soon! So, do you think you can meet me at the office? I'm going to head there in a few minutes."

"Of course I will," I say, already scrambling out of bed.

WHILE I'M GETTING ready, I'm scrolling through tabloid sites. And not liking what I'm seeing.

This is way worse than an arrest notice.

Captive Films definitely needs my help. This has the makings of a publicity nightmare, and it's going to take some brilliance and a whole lot of manipulation on my part to get this under control. I start thinking of ways to spin it.

But as I continue to scroll through the damning photos, I can't help but smile about one thing.

Even though there are numerous photos of the group with random girls, Dawson doesn't appear to have hooked up with anyone.

And that makes me feel happy.

I stop in the kitchen on my way out the door.

Ariela is perched at the breakfast bar eating an omelet made by my chef. I think he has a little crush on her.

"You're up early this morning, Miss Vanessa," he says. "What can I make for you?"

"Just a coffee to go, please," I tell him then turn to Ariela. "Riley was arrested in Vegas last night along with Dawson, Knox, and Jennifer."

"Arrested? Is that why Riley and Dawson had to go to Vegas suddenly? Because of Knox and Jennifer?"

"I'm not sure why, but this doesn't look like a business trip to me." I toss a few of the photos I printed out onto the counter.

She looks at them and lets out a sad sigh. "I thought . . ."

"He was different?"

"Yeah. How could he do this after the night we shared?"

I shrug and say, "He's a man."

"I didn't sleep at all last night. That look he had, on the video we watched of him leaving, it's the same look he had when I told him I wasn't moving here with him. I tried calling him last night. I texted him. Left messages. I have to fly up to the vineyard today and be there all week. If so much wasn't riding on this wedding, I'd go sit at his office until he showed up and get to the bottom of this. I know you think otherwise, but I know in my heart he saw me with Collin."

"I don't mean to sound callous, but if he did, this is the result. A PR nightmare for Captive Films. One that I need to figure out how to fix."

"Can you fix it?"

I shake my head. "At this point, there are too many photos out there to fix. I'm going to have to work on damage control."

"I'm sorry," she says, getting teary. "I shouldn't have come here."

I give her a hug. "It's okay. I'm just a little overwhelmed right now. I promise when I see Riley, I'll tell him the kiss was unwanted. In case he did see."

"Oh, thank you."

"But that's all I can do. It will be up to him to decide if he wants to talk to you about it."

"Thank you. I understand and appreciate it."

CAPTIVE FILMS – SANTA MONICA
KEATYN

WHEN I GET to the office, I start scanning celebrity gossip websites.

The first one I go to, the one with the widest reach, has a video of a very intoxicated Jennifer dancing around a stripper pole.

Make that, dancing around and then falling off a stripper pole.

My phone dings with a text from a board member who

lives on the East Coast.

> *Jennifer Edwards is trending on Twitter. And not in a good way. We can't be associated with someone of this character. You need to cancel her contract immediately.*

I switch over to Twitter and pull up the trending hashtag *#JEdsStripperFail.*

The video from her stripper dance, where she twirls around a pole then face plants, has become a meme. And been shared millions of times already. Jeez, doesn't anyone sleep?

My office phone starts ringing off the hook.

Then my cell rings.

It is another board member, a long standing and vocal one.

"Hi, Walter," I say, trying to sound cheerful.

"You sound too happy this morning. Have you not been online?"

"I just got into the office. It's six a.m. in California."

"Well, then the whole world knows but you. Let me read you a headline. *Captive Films CEO Riley Johnson arrested in Vegas.* And another. *Riley Johnson, CEO of Captive Films—*"

"I'm aware of Riley's arrest. I'll deal with it, Walter. Thanks for alerting me."

"Keatyn, I know Riley is your friend, but this isn't good for our business. I've spoken to some of the other board members and we're in agreement. You need to ask Riley to resign."

"Captive Films is more profitable than it's ever been because of Riley. You and the board know that."

"Does he need to go to rehab? What the hell is going on

with him?"

"It's personal. Don't worry. I'll handle it."

After I end the call, I lay my head on the desk trying to figure out how I'll handle it.

I smell Tyler coming long before I hear him.

"I brought you some coffee," he sings. "I suspect it's going to be a long day."

My stomach starts to churn.

"Um, I've given up coffee for lent."

"It's not lent. Come on, smell it. You know you love it." He waves it across my desk, causing me to gag.

"Please, don't ever bring me coffee again! It's making me sick!" I cry out.

He narrows his eyes at me, takes the coffee out of the office, and comes back with a cup of lemon tea. "My sister drank this when she had morning sickness," he says softly. "She said it helped."

"I'm sorry I yelled at you, Tyler. Please don't tell anyone. We haven't even told our families yet. The crazy thing is I'm sitting here wondering if I announced my pregnancy today if it would give the press something else to think about."

"Well, you know how fickle the press is. They're always moving on to the next big scandal. And if they thought you were pregnant with Knox's love child while engaged to Aiden that would be a pretty big scandal. Can you imagine the headlines?"

"It would take the focus off Riley, Jennifer, and Captive. Make the board happy." I touch my stomach. The thought of using Aiden's and my baby, my pregnancy, to create headlines sickens me.

My cell rings again.

"Shit, it's my grandpa."

"Would you like me to leave?"

"No, it's okay, Tyler." I hand him my laptop. "Look around. Maybe it's not as bad as I think it is."

"Will do, boss," he says, making himself comfortable on the couch.

"Hey, Grandpa," I say into the phone.

"It's a good thing I'm an early riser. Every single board member has called me this morning to raise a ruckus. They all want Riley's head."

"I've heard from a few of them myself. You always have good advice. Tell me what I can do to fix this."

"You can't fix it, Hotshot. He has to. I know he's your best friend, but this is business. Don't let your relationship blind you to what's going on. It'd be different if it was a one-time thing but he's starting to get the kind of publicity Captive doesn't need. Between his relationship with Jennifer, the way he behaved at dinner and, now, this. You can't bury your head in the sand. You have to deal with it. And I'm afraid the board is right."

While I'm talking, Tyler is printing off pictures and laying them across my desk.

Riley shirtless and humping a Greek statue.

Riley and Knox with girls draped all over them in a party bus, cheesing for the camera, their eyes bloodshot and bleary.

Riley naked, sitting on the edge of a hot tub preparing to dive into the middle of about ten topless women.

Knox, wearing a shirt but no pants, being cuffed by a police officer.

Grandpa is still lecturing me, so I have to stifle my laugh. It's pretty funny seeing Knox's naked ass all over the news, especially when it was supposed to be revealed for the first time ever in the next *Trinity* movie. The studio is probably going ballistic about it.

"Your days at Eastbrooke don't mean shit when it comes to business."

Tyler lays a photo of a topless Jennifer sitting on Knox's lap swigging tequila straight from a bottle on top of the ad mock-ups for *Daddy's Angel.*

Something clicks.

"That's it, Tyler. You're brilliant!" I shout.

"Why's Tyler brilliant?" Grandpa asks as Tyler goes, "I am?"

"I have to go, Grandpa. I'll take care of it all. I promise," I say, quickly ending the call.

"What are you going to do?" Tyler asks. "This looks really bad. Like so bad you may need to send them somewhere remote until it all dies down."

"Our senior year at boarding school, we threw different themed parties every other weekend. One was Heaven and Hell."

He tilts his head at me. "I don't get it."

"Shh. I'm still thinking it through. Will you go check on Vanessa? She should be here by now."

I stare at the mock-up some more and suddenly know exactly what to do.

The board won't know what hit them.

The press won't know what hit them.

And, by the time we're done, the board will be telling me to give Riley a raise.

And maybe even suggesting something I've been considering doing since I found out I was pregnant.

VANESSA STROLLS IN, dressed to kill in a black pencil skirt, black spiked Louboutins, and bright red lips that match the bottom of her heels.

"Have you seen all the pictures? How the hell are there so many out there already? I have some ideas for damage control and I think I can get the photos with nudity taken down by calling in some favors, but I think the best thing to do is let it burn out on its own. The last thing we want to do is add more fuel to the fire. We'll make them lay low . . ."

"I just thought of something that might allow us to add fuel to the fire in a good way." I tell her my idea. "But I'm not exactly sure how to spin it. Any ideas on that?"

"YOU TWO COULD rule the world if you put your minds together. And, Vanessa, if you have to face the press today, you'll rock it, girl. Love the shoes," Tyler says, taking notes on all the things we need done today. "Okay, so I'll pull five of our best assistants and have them do nothing but cover the phones today. What do you want our official response to be? And when will you be ready to make a statement to the press?"

"Our official response has to be: *Captive Films has no comment.*" Vanessa says.

Tyler says, "But, I thought—"

"No," Vanessa says, still thinking it through. "For this to work, the press will have to figure it out on their own. We can't even hint at it." She turns to me. "Don't you think so, Keatyn?"

"You're the master at this," I say. "But, yes, I think you're right. If we're going to pull this off, they're going to have to figure it out on their own. Otherwise, they'll see what it really is. Our attempt to manipulate it."

"I feel like the Wizard of Oz," Vanessa laughs. "All

smoke and mirrors."

"How long does it take to bail someone out of jail?" I ask. "We've got to get everyone on the same page. Pray Jennifer doesn't post anything on her social media in the mean time."

"It doesn't take long," Dallas says, strolling in.

"Dallas, what are you doing here? Did RiAnne have the baby already?"

"Ha. False alarm. Doctor told us it will probably be at least two more weeks. My wife is not happy. I decided to let her mother deal with her."

"She keeps saying she wants this baby out of her," I laugh.

"Even with the public relations disaster that is Vegas, it's a whole lot safer here than it is at home right now," Dallas says. "On a side note, I just spoke to Aiden. He's wired the money, they're out, and have taken off. Should be here in about an hour. And he gave them strict orders not to speak to the press or post anything on their social media."

"Another reason I love him," I say. "I want them to come directly here. As in do not pass go. Is Aiden going to meet them at the airport?"

"Yes, and I told him to bring them all here. So how bad is it?"

"Take a look," Vanessa says, pulling him toward my desk and gesturing toward the printouts. "It's bad."

Dallas scratches his neck and grimaces.

"Tyler," I say. "Will you please take all these photos into the board room and get it set up for Vanessa as command central? Then get Lisa, Barry, Dawn, and Craig from the marketing team assembled, privately fill them in on our plan, and have them start working on our list of to dos. We can trust the four of them to help get this all pulled together. But everyone else should be kept in the dark. Have them call in every favor we have to get hair, makeup, and a photographer here within the hour. We'll also need them to pull together the guest list and get the invitations out. And, somehow, we need to cast Matthew today. Anyone have ideas on how we could do that?"

Dallas smiles and raises his hand. "Jake Worth. I golfed with him last week. He's got offers on the table but he's tired of playing the good guy. And he's free now."

"Oh, he'd be perfect! I don't know why I didn't think of him in the first place. I'll call him right now. Dallas, will you stay in here while I do? I want to discuss something else with you."

"Sure," he says, taking a seat as Vanessa and Tyler rush off.

I grab my cell phone and press Jake's number.

"Hey, Monroe," he says, calling me by my fake last name from boarding school. Jake was the first boy I met when I arrived at Eastbrooke and we became fast friends. He played my love interest in our high school drama production, was Dawson's best friend, and made his big screen debut playing my boyfriend in *A Day at the Lake 2*. He's done numerous romantic comedies since then, where he always gets the girl.

"Sorry for such an early call, but I'm sitting here with Dallas and he tells me you're looking to play the bad boy."

"Do you have something for me?"

"We do. But due to some extenuating circumstances, we'd have to ask you to come in today, sign the contract, and be in a photo shoot. We'll also need you available most of the week for some other stuff I can't talk about yet."

"Tell me about the role. Have you cast anyone else?"

"The project is called *Daddy's Angel.* It's about a young woman whose father is a minister at the local church. He believes his daughter, Angel, is still a virgin and is looking for a young man to court then marry her."

"Court her?"

"Yeah, like the old-fashioned way, sort of. There are lots of rules. Like no holding hands until you are engaged. No kissing until your wedding day. Chaperones when you are together. You would play Jackson, the town's bad boy. What Daddy doesn't know is that Angel lives a very promiscuous double life and Jackson is her favorite plaything. Jennifer Edwards will be playing Angel and Knox Daniels will be playing Nathan, the guy who Daddy brings in to court Angel. Of course, Nathan believes Angel is a good girl virgin and while Daddy thinks Nathan's a church going man, he's a bad boy too. He only wants to marry Angel to get control of some land Daddy owns that has lots of oil under it. And he thinks he can do that by getting Angel to fall in love with him."

"Two bad boys. That sounds like every woman's dream."

"Based on the gross from your last film, I think *you're* every woman's dream, Jake."

"Do I get the girl in the end?"

"No."

"Ha! Even better. Did you write the script?"

"Yes."

"Then I'm in."

I give Dallas a thumbs-up.

"Can you be at our office, like now?"

"Sure thing."

"Awesome. You'll meet with Dallas first, talk contract, and then you'll go straight to a photo shoot with Knox and Jennifer."

"She's a cutie. I'm excited to work with her. She kissed me at the Oscars."

I laugh. "I think she kissed everyone. She'll be excited to work with you. And thanks, Jake."

"Anytime, Monroe. See you soon."

I hang up and look down at my cell. More missed calls. More texts from board members.

"We need to talk about Riley," I say with a sigh to Dallas. "The board wants me to fire him."

"Ariela has him all messed up."

"I know. I feel bad."

"Don't. I think it's about time he dealt with it."

"Thanks, Dallas. That makes me feel better."

"Keatyn, Vegas and how Riley has been behaving is on him. So are you going to fire him?"

"I do want to make some changes," I say.

Then I tell him what I plan to do.

"HOW DO YOU think Riley will take it?" I ask Dallas, nervously.

"You kinda have him by the balls right now."

"I don't want that though. Grandpa is right. Working with friends can be tricky."

"It will be interesting to see Riley's reaction."

"You're going to make me cry, Dallas."

"Better than making you puke," he says with a laugh, getting up. "I'm gonna go get Jake's contract ready. Do you need me to make some calls to the board members? Buy you some time?"

"No, they can wait with everyone else. I mean, what's the worst thing they can do? Even if they all get pissed and sell their stock, I own the majority. I did a hostile takeover once," I say, remembering how I bought out the company that became Captive Films from my stalker. "No way I'd ever let our investment become vulnerable. They'll just have to trust I'll do what's best for Captive."

"True. They just want their egos stroked."

"I should have a dirty comeback for that, Dallas, but I'm too tired."

"You look tired. Have you eaten this morning? You're growing a baby. It takes a lot of calories. Have Tyler order in some food. We're going to be here all day. Wait, aren't you supposed to be on set?"

"I was, but they cancelled my call time because, well, because Knox was in jail."

CAPTIVE FILMS — SANTA MONICA
RILEY

AIDEN PICKED US up at the airport and announced that he'd been instructed to take us straight to Captive Films.

We're entering in the back way, through the parking garage to Keatyn's private entrance.

"I'm not going in there!" Jennifer cries. "I'm a mess!"

"I second that," Knox says.

I keep my mouth shut. I got kicked out of boarding school my freshman year because of an incident involving an older girl, a Homecoming float, and a lot of alcohol, sex, and nakedness. I feel like that freshman boy again, waiting in the principal's office for my parents to arrive, and wondering how much trouble I'm going to be in.

"I don't really feel good," Knox says, cracking the window.

Dawson punches him in the shoulder. "You were feeling good last night."

"Does anyone even remember last night?" Jennifer asks, holding her head.

"Don't worry," Aiden says. "I'm told there are *plenty* of photos to fill the gaps in your memory."

Jennifer's eyes get big. "Are you serious? There are pictures?"

"Yes. Your fun last night is this morning's publicity nightmare. Keatyn started getting calls from board members at five this morning."

"Shit," Jennifer and I both say, slumping down in our seats.

WE ARRIVE THROUGH the back elevator and are lined up in the board room like we're going in front of a firing squad. I see through the glass that Vanessa is marching toward us.

And she looks pissed.

"I can't take her today," I mutter.

"Take who?" Knox whispers.

"Vanessa. She's gonna yell at me about my image. I'm so fucking hung over."

Vanessa marches in the room like a general, commanding our attention. She struts straight up to my brother, grabs him by his shirt, and kisses him straight on the lips.

"Uh, um, what was that for?" he mumbles, still recovering from the shock of it.

"When you were in Vegas, did you have sex with anyone?"

"Uh, no," he replies.

I roll my eyes at him, wondering why the hell he didn't. He had his choice of hot women.

Vanessa gives him a radiant smile. "That's what the kiss was for."

He grins at her like a lovesick puppy, making me both want to puke at the sweetness of it and feel jealous at the same time.

"Speaking of kisses," she says, coming to stand directly in front of me. "For the record, Ariela's husband showed up unexpected, begged her to come home, and then kissed her. And in case you happened to see it when you came to pick her up and your stupid male brain thought otherwise, the kiss was unwanted."

I look at the floor, realizing that this whole mess was because I jumped to a conclusion.

"Are you serious?" Jennifer groans. "She didn't kiss him? Riley, you're such an idiot."

"I'm not an idiot. What the fuck was I supposed to think? His car was in the driveway. She's at the door, holding her heels in her hand, giving him a kiss goodbye. I didn't just think she kissed him. It looked to me like they just had sex and she was shooing him out the door before I got there. What do we even know about them anyway? Maybe this is all just a ploy to weasel me out of my money."

"Right now, Ariela is the absolute least of your worries, Riley. We have a shit storm of bad publicity we have to deal with it. And blame Ariela all you want, but this is about you. Your life. Your career." She stops chewing me out and appraises us. "Jeez, you all look like hell." She points toward the conference table. "And somehow, I doubt what you're going to see here will make you feel any better. Take a look at all the photos we've found on the web so far. Jennifer, you may be especially interested in looking at the laptop. You are currently trending on Twitter with a meme made from video footage taken of you at a strip club."

Jennifer looks sick as she sits down at the table and clicks.

"Oh my god! What an epic fail!" She screams, then laughs, but then breaks down into tears. "My parents are going to kill me."

Keatyn and Tyler come into the room, laden with bags. When they spread the food out, I see that it's my favorite breakfast. The combination I taught Keatyn to love when she first tried it on my seventeenth birthday. Chicken and waffles.

"I figured you could use some hangover food," Keatyn declares. "Why don't you eat while Vanessa and I fill you in on what's going to happen next. As you can see, your fun night in Vegas is all over the press. What you don't know about are all the calls I've been receiving from our Board of Directors. They're calling for your heads. They want me to cancel Knox and Jennifer's contracts and fire both Riley and Dawson. Immediately."

I choke down my food when I hear that the board wants me fired.

I know now why she ordered chicken and waffles. Because this is my last meal at Captive.

It's even worse than I imagined.

JENNIFER IS SHOVELING food in her mouth while looking through the photos. She holds up one where she wrapped a scarf around her head, tied her shirt up in the middle, and has a fake parrot on her shoulder. "When was this? I don't remember this."

Dawson answers. "After the first club, we toured the Strip in a party bus. You were convinced if you looked like a pirate you could get on the ship at Treasure Island."

"And this?" she asks, holding up a photo of her on a thrill ride.

"That's the X-Scream at the Stratosphere," Dawson says.

"Did we all ride it?"

"Yeah, we went before the second club. Thank god, you were impatient and volunteered to go single. You came back covered in puke. I think I bought the picture. It's classic, we can download it if you want," Dawson says, eating and laughing.

Vanessa shoots him an evil eye.

"I mean, at the time it was funny."

"I thought it was funny," Knox says. "I remember doing all that. The second strip club is when things start to get blurry."

"I'd like to try to piece together a schedule of your night," Keatyn interjects. "Tyler, will you start writing this all down."

"How will that help?" Dawson asks.

"We need to know everything that happened if we're going to have any chance of dealing with this appropriately," Vanessa states. She may be an ice queen, but she knows her stuff. "Dawson, you seem to remember the most. Let's start with you."

"On the plane, we pre-partied. Drank a lot of champagne. We got to Vegas. Checked into our suite. It was the coolest place I've ever seen. I didn't know they even had suites like it. There was a round bed that rotated. A fireman's pole. Remember sliding down it?" he says excitedly.

Everyone nods as I remember what Jennifer told me on the bed. That I should care that she was fucking Knox.

When did I stop caring?

After Ariela.

"Oh, gosh," Jennifer says, holding up a photo. "Knox, why were we humping Roman statues?"

"You said you wanted to have a threesome," Knox says, laughing.

I'd be laughing too if I wasn't waiting for this to be over so Keatyn could fire me.

"Do you remember stripping off your skirt to skinny dip in the fountain?" Knox asks her. "You said if throwing a penny in and making a wish for love was supposed to work, that immersing your whole body would ensure happiness."

"There's a photo of that too," Tyler says, rummaging through photos to find the correct one and then handing it to Jennifer.

"Okay, so we have fire pole sliding, a strip club, a roller coaster ride, statue humping, and attempted skinny dipping," Vanessa says. "What else?"

"Then we got politely asked to leave the Forum shops and to never return," Dawson says. "After that, we took the party bus to strip club number two. We did shots on the way there."

"This must be at strip club number two," Knox says, holding up a photo of a topless Jennifer giving him a lap dance. And another one of them making out.

Jennifer holds up another photo, comparing them. "This one looks like it was taken at the same place, but because we're both shirtless, it gives the impression that we're naked and having sex. My parents are going to fucking kill me. Not to mention my agent. And I don't even want to talk to my publicist. Remind me to never go to Vegas with you all again."

"That goes for me too," Dawson says. "Although, I do remember having fun."

"I remember having fun too," Jennifer says, holding up a photo of her surrounded by barely dressed waitresses. "But I just don't understand. Where did the press get all these photos?"

"You took a lot of photos," Knox says. "I do remember that. You were obsessed with it. You said an epic night needs a record. So you could remember everything you'd probably forget."

"And you gave me your phone and made me video you on the stripper pole," Dawson admits.

"Well, here's a fun photo," Tyler interrupts with a smirk on his face, holding a stack of photos out for all of us to see. "Jennifer, you were a lovely drunken bride. Which one of you was the lucky groom?"

Jennifer's face goes white.

"What?!" Jennifer screeches as she grabs the photos out of Tyler's hand. Looking at the first one, she says, "Oh! Look at me with Elvis! Ohmigawd that photo is priceless! But I was probably just dressing up like the pirate thing. No way we got married."

Knox holds out a manila envelope. As he dumps the contents of it, I notice little beads of sweat have formed on his forehead. Knox rarely sweats.

Two shiny silver wedding bands clang onto the table.

"Oh fuck!" Jennifer groans. "Knox? What the fuck? Did we get married? I was joking when I said let's get married in Vegas. Oh my god." She flips to the next photo. "Look at me in this one. I'm in a veil. I have that silver ring on my finger and the other in my hand! I'm giving Elvis a thumbs-up! And, ohmigawd, look at this one. Knox, we're at the altar, kissing!"

"I remember going to a wedding," Dawson admits. "And, Jennifer, I remember you throwing a bouquet."

"Did you sign anything?" Knox asks Dawson, clearly shaken by this. "If you were our witness, you would have signed something. Now that I think about it, I do remember being at a chapel. I was on the steps and worried I was going to puke and ruin the wedding. But I think it was someone else's wedding."

"I remember crashing a wedding," I interject. I haven't said a word this whole time. I'm afraid to open my mouth, but Knox's face is getting so red, I'm worried he might have a stroke.

"Oh, me too, now that you say that," Dawson confirms. "I think you and Jennifer stood up for someone. They said it would be an honor. Then, I think later, Jennifer took her veil."

Knox lets out a big breath of air. "Dodged that bullet," he says, obviously relieved.

"Wasn't there a wedding party on our party bus?" Dawson asks. "Didn't we invite them back to the suite?"

"Yes! I remember that!" Jennifer says. "I puked in the party bus, and the bride told me that was the best way to cure a hangover. That I should just stay drunk. So I started drinking again."

Tyler hands her another photo.

She studies it and then turns it toward us. "Okay, so I know I was drunk, but how in the fuck could the press have gotten this? It's a selfie. See my arm?"

"You probably used the bride's phone and she sent it in," Keatyn states. "I mean if Knox Daniels and Jennifer Edwards were at my wedding, I'd post about it."

"Where is your phone?" Vanessa asks Jennifer.

"I think I lost it," she says.

"Or maybe that's our answer. Maybe someone found it," Vanessa suggests.

"I did take the passcode off last night because I kept screwing it up. Shit. I'm an idiot."

"Did you get an envelope at the police station like Knox did?" Keatyn asks her.

"Oh, yeah! I did. Let me see what's in there. Everyone should look. Maybe there are more clues."

"I think the internet has more than enough clues," Vanessa deadpans.

Jennifer dumps the contents then screeches, "My phone!" She looks at it and goes, "Ohmygawd, I'm down to one percent. I need a charger, stat!"

Tyler runs out of the office and rushes back in with one, plugging it into the wall behind her.

"You're a life saver—oh shit, it just died."

"Plug it in, anyway," Tyler says.

She leans back in the chair, staring at her phone, willing it to life.

I take another helping of chicken and pick at it. The silence in the room is freaking me out. I already looked at my phone, saw it was dead, and decided to leave it that way. Anyone who needs to reach me can call the office. I'm sure Ariela found the flowers and left me a message. I don't want to know what she said.

I just don't want to know.

"It's awake and loading now," Jennifer says.

We watch her hit buttons on her phone, her eyes getting bigger by the second.

"Um, shit . . ." she mutters.

"What?" Vanessa prods.

"Besides the seventeen missed calls from my parents, it appears that I sent my ex-boyfriend exactly sixty one texts last night."

She bangs her head on the desk and leaves it there.

"Your ex, huh?" Knox says, "You were texting him while you were with me?"

"I'm sorry I just—"

"You just what?"

"I wanted to make the jerk jealous. I wanted him to see that I could party too."

"Which means you still care about him," Knox states.

"No, I just . . ." Jennifer stutters. Then she lays her head on the desk dramatically and whispers, "I sent him all the photos."

"Well, that solves the mystery of how the press got them," Knox says, fuming. "Why in the hell would you send photos like that to Parker Hudson after the way he treated you in the press?"

"I don't know. I was drunk, maybe?!" she says. "Jeez, can this day get any worse?"

AND IT DOES get worse when Dallas enters the room with a sheet of paper and starts reading from it.

"I just received the list of charges from the Vegas PD. Let's see, we have a plethora to choose from. Public intoxication. Public lewdness. Indecent exposure."

"We were having a naked parade," Jennifer admits. "It seemed like a fun idea at the time."

"It looked fun," Dallas says, "based on the photos. And we have destruction of hotel property. Disorderly conduct. And my favorite, impersonating a police officer."

"My bad," Knox says.

"How did you manage to do that naked?" Dallas asks him.

"Based on the photos, I was simply pantless. And I may have told them I was undercover and if they didn't leave they would blow my cover."

"That didn't go over so well, I'm assuming?"

"No. Then I tried to tell them that I meant I played one on TV."

"Have you ever been on TV?" Dallas asks.

"Seriously? You don't remember the cameo I did? Everyone says I fucking stole the show. How can you not remember that?"

"I wasn't drunk enough to participate in the naked parade," Dawson says, trying to suck up.

"But, you were apparently drunk enough to bribe an officer—let's see—to *make it go away*," Dallas states.

"I just meant we could pay extra to the hotel. He took it the wrong way."

Dallas shakes his head. "I'll deal with the legal aspects of the charges. What's more important is how we deal with the press. I'm pretty sure the whole world has seen the photos."

"But I think we've all been at this long enough to know one thing," Keatyn says.

"That no publicity is bad publicity," Vanessa finishes.

"What do you mean? There's no way *this* can be turned around," Jennifer says, facing the laptop toward everyone and allowing them to see the video of her twirling, mostly naked, around the stripper pole, only to fall flat on her face.

"It can be if we act fast," Vanessa disagrees, holding the mock-up of a *Daddy's Angel* ad. "And *this* is how we're going to do it."

"I don't get it," Jennifer says, echoing my own thoughts.

"You don't really have to get it," Dallas states. "You just have to do exactly what we say. And, if you don't, you and Knox will both be out of a contract."

Knox, who is shoving food in his mouth, doesn't seem all that fazed by this. But he and Keatyn are used to being in the tabloids.

I'm not.

"Jennifer," Keatyn says. "Hair and makeup are on their way. We're going to shoot this ad today, with you in it. I'm sure you don't feel great, but you're gonna have to suck it up. Tomorrow, we're going to leak a couple of those photos to the press, with the rumor of an announcement to come."

"What announcement?" Jennifer asks.

"We're throwing a party this weekend," Vanessa replies. "And your attendance is mandatory."

"Um, not this weekend," Keatyn says. "Tomorrow night. Riley will be busy this weekend."

The way Keatyn says it, makes me cringe. What is she going to make me do this weekend? Is she firing me? Will I be packing up my office this weekend?

What would I do without this place?

It's my life. My love. My dream.

Hard to believe one stupid night in Vegas could ruin everything.

Vegas needs to change their slogan, because what happens in Vegas clearly does *not* stay there.

How did my life get so out of control?

I have a vision of Ariela kissing her husband and know

exactly why.

She's the one who I dreamed of sharing this with. It's a strange twist of fate to think she could also be the one who destroys it.

"Dawson," Vanessa says. "We'll need your help getting this all set up. Plan on working nonstop with me."

Damn, if a smirk doesn't cross my brother's face.

"So I hope you're all up for another big party," Vanessa says.

"I can't do that again," Knox begs. "I'm too old. I don't recover well."

Keatyn ignores his pleas. "So, the party is where we will officially announce the *Daddy's Angel* project. The photo shoot we do today will become teasers for the series, simply branded with a tag line and the series name. Knox, you will be included in the shoot for these teasers as will Jake Worth, who we've signed on to play Jackson. Riley, you'll be in on this too."

When she says my name, I perk up. "You want *me* in the photos?"

"Yes, you have to be part of the cast now. You're going to play Bobby, the church's photographer, who would like to exploit Angel's body on his secret porn site. It's a cameo role."

Knox wipes his mouth with a napkin, stands up, and pulls Keatyn into a hug. "Sugar, I taught you well."

"What the hell are you talking about?" I ask. "I don't understand how a party will help."

"The party will be a *Purity* Party," Vanessa states. "Everyone in attendance will be required to dress in white. All the decor will be white. Drinks will be white. But Knox, Jake, and Riley will be dressed in black. Jennifer in a hot red dress."

"And once you throw the Purity Party," Knox says, "it will make Vegas look like it was the hellcat party and nothing more than a publicity stunt."

"Exactly," Keatyn and Vanessa say, grinning.

And I have to hand it to them. "That's fucking brilliant," I mutter.

"If you can actually pull this off," Jennifer says to Vanessa, "I'm firing my PR firm and hiring you. I mean, if you'd have me as a client."

Vanessa walks over and gives Jennifer a hug in an almost motherly way, which surprises me. I've never seen her act that way before.

"Alright," Keatyn says, clapping her hands together. "Jennifer and Knox, Tyler will escort you to the photo shoot now. Dawson, do whatever Vanessa needs help with. And, Riley, I need you come to my office with me and Dallas."

Everyone does as they're told.

I'm afraid to move.

The fact that she wouldn't say whatever it is in front of everyone means it's bad. I hope the cameo in *Daddy's Angel* pays well. It may be my only job soon.

I SIT DOWN on Keatyn's couch.

She plops down next to me. "How are you?"

"I'm fine," I lie.

"No, you're not, Riley. Last night was a disaster. We're so freaking lucky we have this project or I don't know how we'd get out of this mess. We need to pray this works, and we need to convince more than just the public. The board of directors wants me to fire you."

"We've just had our best quarter ever. Our best year

ever," I counter.

"Even Grandpa is on my ass. He suggested sending you to rehab. After your behavior at the vineyard combined with this, he is afraid our friendship is going be the company's downfall."

"Is it?" I ask, trying not to cry.

Yes, big, tough Riley feels like he could cry. I don't want to let Keatyn down. Captive Films started with the three of us: Dallas, Keatyn, and me. We've been best friends since Eastbrooke.

There's nothing better than working with the people you love.

And I let them both down.

Fuck.

"I'm sorry," I say, hanging my head.

Keatyn puts her hand on my leg. "Riley, there's something I need you to do with me."

"With *us*," Dallas adds.

"What?"

"We're going to Eastbrooke's homecoming this weekend."

"But I thought you had to work and couldn't go this year?"

"I begged the director to do some rescheduling."

"And if I can't?" I ask tentatively.

"If you don't go, nothing will happen," Dallas says.

"I'm not firing you, Riley. We couldn't do this without you," Keatyn adds. "What you should ask is what will happen if you go."

"What will happen if I go?"

She leans closer to me, tears filling her eyes. "If you do it, if you'll go back with us and get the closure you need, at the next board meeting, I'll be announcing that I'm stepping down and promoting you to CEO *and* Chairman of the Board."

I blink my eyes, not believing what I just heard.

"What?" I ask, overcome with emotion.

"I've been thinking about it for a while, Riley. You deserve it."

I reach over and pull her into a tight hug.

She still believes in me and I'm so grateful.

"Are you crying?" Dallas asks.

"Shut the fuck up," I say, wiping away a tear.

"Pussy," he teases then laughs. "You were really afraid she was going to fire you, weren't you?"

"Yeah, I was." I'm still hugging Keatyn tightly.

She whispers in my ear. "You're Riley Johnson. The boy who wanted to protect me even though you didn't know I needed protecting. I don't care what happens. *We're* what makes this company successful. The three of us."

"Shit," Dallas drawls and joins our hug. "Now you're gonna make me cry."

ASHER VINEYARDS—SONOMA COUNTY
ARIELA

BASED ON WHAT happened in Vegas, I'm certain Riley saw Collin kiss me. And since he's not returning my calls, I'm going to prove to him in another way how much I still love him.

As I look around the vineyard, I know how I'm going to do it.

By making Keatyn's wedding perfection.

So much of my future here in California feels like it's riding on this wedding.

If it's perfect, maybe people here will want to hire me. If it's perfect, maybe Keatyn won't kick me out of her life when she hears that I kissed Collin. Maybe if it's perfect, it will make Riley happy simply because Keatyn will be happy.

They've been best friends for so long. When Riley and I first started dating, I was jealous of how close they were.

And I'm jealous of how close they all still are. Dallas, Keatyn, Riley, Aiden, Maggie, and Logan are all still best friends.

I missed out on so much.

If I can pull off the perfect wedding, it will show them all how sorry I am that I walked away from our friendships.

And I need the distraction of planning the wedding to keep me off the internet.

Every time I checked, I found a new photo of Riley's night in Vegas.

The last one was a mug shot with an article that mentioned his arrest.

After that, I shut my laptop, got ready, and headed here.

Maggie greets me at the business office. "Have you seen all the crazy news about Riley, Knox, and Jennifer?"

"Yeah," I say sadly.

"What's the real story?"

"I don't know for sure. Vanessa left for Captive's offices really early and I haven't heard from her since."

"Aiden said it's quite the publicity nightmare, but that Keatyn already has a plan to turn it around. She and Knox are brilliant when it comes to manipulating the press."

"Riley and I were supposed to go on a date last night," I admit. "When he got there, I think he saw Collin kiss me."

"Oh my. Is that why Riley went to Vegas?"

"I think so. Vanessa has video surveillance, so I got to see the look on Riley's face when he left—" I hang my head.

"What?" Maggie says.

"It reminded me of graduation day. When I told him I wasn't coming to California with him. We had an amazing night together and we were planning to go to Eastbrooke's homecoming this weekend . . ."

"I think you should still go. Without him. It's sad. We always go, but Keatyn had to work, so Aiden booked us a Moon Wish fundraiser."

"So why do you think I should go alone?"

"It might be nice to be there by yourself. I mean, obviously, there will be a lot of people, but none of your close high school friends. I just think it might help you get some closure."

"That's why Riley wanted us to go back."

Maggie's cell rings, so she answers and tells them to send someone up.

"The event rep is here. Just think about it."

"I will, Maggie. Thanks."

"You know, once word gets out that you've planned Keatyn's wedding, you will have more jobs than you'll know what to do with. I'm not sure what you want to do, but we're looking to hire an event coordinator."

"I thought you already had one?"

"We do. Here onsite. This is a different role. We do fundraising events all over the world and have been contracting planners in each location. We'd like to have someone in-house to be in charge of all those events."

"So it would be for Moon Wish?"

"Yes. Meaning you could live anywhere in the world you

wanted and still do the job."

"Wow. That would be amazing. Why don't you do it?"

"I'm doing it right now and it's too much with everything that goes on here. Not only are we a working vineyard, we have a restaurant, a wine tasting room, and a store. And we host about ten events a week." She gives me a hug. "I'll get out of your hair and let you get to work. Text me if you need anything or if you hear from Riley."

"I will," I say, grabbing my phone and holding it up.

The second she leaves the room, I check to see if I have a message from Riley.

I don't.

CAPTIVE FILMS—SANTA MONICA
VANESSA

AFTER KEATYN DISMISSES us, I march down to Dawson's office. He's slowly following behind me.

Once inside his office, he slides closer. "That kiss in the board room was hot."

"You smell like Vegas; a mixture of alcohol, stale cigars, and puke. You need a shower."

He gives me a naughty grin, puts his nose next to my neck and sniffs me. "You smell too. I think you need to shower with me."

"I smell like expensive perfume. And, in case you didn't notice, we're in the middle of a crisis, Dawson. I don't have time for a shower. I have to be back in the boardroom shortly."

He runs his hand up the back of my neck and into my hair. "Fine," he says. "I'll shower. You watch."

"I'm not going to stay here and watch you shower," I say, as I sit myself on an ottoman that happens to have a perfect view of the all glass shower. "We have way too much to do."

He starts stripping off his clothes and I forget all about work.

He smirks at me, knowing I can't take my eyes off his gorgeous body. When he slowly walks past me, naked, just to put his dirty clothes in the laundry bag, I know he's messing with me.

"I am, however, going to stay here and give you updates *while* you shower. That will be a good use of our time."

He gives me a nod, steps into the shower, then turns on the water and leans back, letting the water rush over his face.

I try to focus on my phone, which keeps vibrating with emails. "They've secured a location for the—" Dawson squeezes soap into his hand and lathers it all over himself, his hand sliding down washboard abs and then further down between his legs. I bite my lip. "—Purity Party. Guess where it's going to be at?"

"Where?"

"An old church that is now an event space."

"That fits the theme," he says, turning to face me and giving me a full view of—everything. "Who thought of that?"

"Tyler, actually. He went to a party there last year."

"He seems like he runs the place," Dawson laughs.

"He pretty much does. Even though his official title is executive assistant, everyone here knows the pecking order is Keatyn, Riley, Dallas, and then Tyler."

"He's interviewing assistants for me," he says, his arm muscles flexing as he lathers up his hair. When he leans back to rinse out the shampoo, his hips jut forward, giving me a clear view of his dick.

I lower my head and close my eyes. I need to focus on work or I'm going to be stripping off my clothes and joining him.

The sound of the shower being turned off makes me look up.

Dawson is drying off.

I touch my suit pocket, knowing I've been waiting for the right moment all morning.

He steps out of the shower with a towel wrapped around his waist.

I stand up and quickly close the gap between us, my lips meeting his forcefully. He sets me on the bathroom counter, pushes up my skirt, and pulls off my underwear as I slip my hand under the towel and stroke him.

He's completely hard and ready.

I reach into my pocket and pull out a condom. "Put this on," I say into his lips. "So it won't be messy."

I can feel his grin against my lips before he shoves his tongue deeper into my mouth, practically devouring me. I hear paper tear and then he's inside me.

Filling the need that has been burning since I studied the photos and realized he didn't sleep with anyone.

I wrap my legs around his waist and my arms around his neck, hanging on tightly as I thrust against him with equal force.

My orgasm is sudden and practically explosive. I pull him in tighter and call out his name while he continues to slam me against the counter until he comes. His ability to make me feel nearly animalistic still delights and shocks me.

And as hot as it is, all the emotions I feel for him are still there, quite possibly burning brighter than before.

Because, now, I know I can trust him.

CAPTIVE FILMS—SANTA MONICA
DAWSON

"IT'S NEARLY SIX," I tell Vanessa, who is still tapping away on her computer. "We've been working non-stop. It's time for a break." I move behind her and start massaging her neck.

"Oh, wow. That feels amazing," she purrs. "So, let's talk about Vegas."

"Haven't we talked about it enough already?" I say with a chuckle.

"Not about you specifically," she says.

"Well me, specifically, loves that you brought a condom. Did you plan on attacking me in my office?"

"Maybe I thought about it. But that's not what I mean."

"I know the night was a bit of a cluster, but it was fun. I haven't let loose like that in—well, a long time. I think the last time I was drunk was the night we got pregnant with Harlow. Because when you have children, you have to be responsible. Like what if I was drinking and one of the kids needed to go to the hospital?"

"You call an ambulance?" she says flatly. I can't tell if she's kidding or making fun of me.

"You know what I mean."

"I do. I'm just teasing you a little. I love that your children are so important to you. But back to Vegas."

"Vanessa, why don't you just tell me what you want to know. It would be a lot easier than me trying to guess."

She smiles but I see the pain in her eyes.

"Actually, I think I know. You want to know why I didn't sleep with anyone."

"We don't have any kind of an agreement about that. You could have," she says, but it's what she isn't saying that gets to me. I know her ex cheated on her, but I get the feeling it was more than that. I remember her saying she wore red lipstick to feel confident. Whatever he did to her, rocked her to the core, and that's something I understand.

I pull her into my arms. "I'm smart enough not to fuck up a good thing."

"Is that what we are? A *good* thing?" she replies bitchily.

"You seem upset by my word choice. What is your definition of a good thing?"

"For most men that would mean sex with no strings."

"I guess I'm not most men then. I meant that I think we're good together, and not just in bed." I cup her face tenderly. I want her to know she's more—way more—than just sex to me. If it weren't for the fact that it's only been a week, I'd tell her right now that I'm in love with her. As we end our kiss, I try to convey with my eyes the depth of my feelings.

She holds my gaze and then softly says, "Dawson, I lo— I um, *lost* something. I just realized. Um, I'll be right back."

Then she rushes out of my office.

What the hell?

CAPTIVE FILMS—SANTA MONICA
VANESSA

"GOD, WHAT AM I going to do now?" I say to myself,

marching down the hall.

Keatyn yells at me. "What happened? Did Jennifer break the Internet? Although, that wouldn't necessarily be a bad thing."

I let out a frustrated sigh and walk into her office. "No, everything is fine—well, as good as can be expected under the circumstances. It's Dawson. He and I—we seem so— and then I almost—"

"Almost what?"

"Dawson and I are sort of seeing each other. And we're having incredibly hot sex. It's amazing. So amazingly good." I roll my eyes. "I'm an attorney and a successful business woman, for goodness sakes, and just listen to me. I sound like a teenager. But he *is* amazing. And the sex—my god— the sex is beyond phenomenal. The best *ever*. But it's not just that. He's so sweet and sincere and sweet."

"And that's a problem?"

"I asked him about Vegas. Why he didn't sleep with anyone."

"What'd he say?"

"That it was because of me. That he didn't want to fuck up a good thing. He thinks we're a good thing. And then he gave me this kiss—" I cross my arms in front of my chest and hug myself. "—that was so full of emotion that I almost said *I love you*. I wasn't even thinking, it just naturally came out. I said I lo—realized what I was about to say then said I lost something and got the hell out of there. What the fuck is wrong with me?"

"It's okay if you're in love with him, Vanessa. I loved Aiden when I first met him. Your heart knows, so don't let your head get in the way."

"I feel stupid and lovesick. Hell, even my teen self would

tell me that I'm clearly his rebound. His entry back into society as an eligible bachelor."

"Vanessa, you went through a lot—just like Dawson did. And after two years of suffering in your own ways, you're both ready to love again. I'm happy for you. *You* should be happy for you."

"If I would have let the *I love you* tumble out of my mouth, do you think he would've run the other way?"

Keatyn chuckles and gives me a smirk. "I don't know. Maybe I should ask his best friend to ask him if he likes you back."

I roll my eyes. "Shut up. No. We are adults. I'm leaving this conversation now and getting back to work. Obviously, I have a lot of work to do. It would be huge for me to add Jennifer to my list of clients."

As I'm walking out, she says, "So, don't ask?"

I turn around and hold the door frame. "No, I'm being ridiculous. I'll ask him myself."

"Hey, wait a second," she says.

I rush back to her desk. "Do you know something? Did he say something about me?"

"Oh my. You do have it bad," she laughs. "Actually, I just thought of another way you could sway Jennifer."

I plop down in the chair in front of her desk. "Shit."

"You say it like falling in love is a bad thing."

"It is."

"Enjoy it, Vanessa. Picture yourself married to him five years from now. You don't want to look back and realize you missed out on feeling this way because you were being cynical."

"I saw the movie, Keatyn. You have no room to talk."

"I was seventeen and had extenuating circumstances."

"So do I."

She raises an eyebrow at me.

"We all have baggage," I simply state.

"Well," she says with a laugh. "You're over the weight limit. You need to take a bunch of it out, throw it away, and just take a carry-on with you."

"When was the last time you flew commercial?" I ask her.

"Like, never. Okay, I was probably ten."

"Exactly, which means you know I can take as many damn bags as I want."

"But do you need them?" she says softly.

"What do you mean?"

"Neither of you need the baggage anymore."

"How is it in one sentence you've managed to sum up everything my shrink has been trying to tell me for the past year?" I ask.

"Because I know how freeing it is when all the baggage disappears. Pretend Dawson is an impulse trip. Like we just decided to go to Italy, right now, and we'll buy everything we need once we get there. Have you thought anymore about selling the house?"

I sigh. "I can't sell it, Keatyn, it's *so* beautiful."

"It's like living in a museum. Have you ever curled up on the living room couch and marathon-watched movies? Only getting up to pee or get more snacks?"

"Um, no. I have a huge home theater. Why would I do that?"

She frowns at me and seems to change tactics when she asks, "Do you like the decor we chose for Dawson's beach house? Or were you too busy having sex to notice?"

"I noticed," I say, rolling my eyes. "It's beautiful. So

comfortable and inviting."

She holds her hands up, gesturing that I just answered my own question.

"Fine. I'll think about it," I agree, getting up to leave. "Wait, you were gonna tell me something about Jennifer."

"Oh, that's right. I was just thinking about her ex, Parker Hudson. He's a little shit. I really can't believe he leaked all sixty-one photos."

"He probably got a lot of money for them. And since she freely sent them to him, she has no legal recourse. It worked out well for us though. You know other photos would have come out, but they would have trickled out day by day. Parker shot his wad all at once. No one could ever suggest we planted them."

"Right. And once everyone believes Vegas was the Sinner's Party, there's no reason you couldn't let it leak that Jennifer *purposely* sent them to him. That she was acting— pretending to be drunk—because she knew he would be an asshole and sell them."

"So, one point for Jennifer. In the scheme of things, that doesn't really help, does it?"

Keatyn hands me an envelope. "A good friend delivered this to me today. I've been trying to decide what to do with it."

I pull the photo out and quickly shut my eyes. "Oh! You could have warned me they were having sex in the picture. Mentally prepared me."

"I didn't want to prepare you. I wanted it to shock you just like it will shock Parker's fans. I've never heard a single rumor about him playing for both teams. And look closer at the photo. It's not *just* gay sex. It's a full blown gay orgy."

"Where the hell did you get this?"

"I'm afraid I can't reveal my source."

"Which means, Sander," I surmise, based on the fact she is still close to the actor, who she dated in high school well before he came out of the closet. "I'm really surprised Sander would give you this. He didn't come out of the closet until a few years ago."

"*Whoever* sent this to me believes that it doesn't matter what Parker's sexual orientation is. The guy's a dick. He suggested showing it to Parker as a means of persuading him to admit to the press that he shared Jennifer's photos because he's an asshole, and to ensure he doesn't give her any more shit."

"That's sorta blackmail. I'm shocked, Keatyn."

"We're persuading him to be nice to one person. I'd hardly call that blackmail."

"Should we show Jennifer?"

"No, I think she's had enough for the last twenty-four hours."

"You must be talking about me," Knox says, knocking on Keatyn's door. "Just want to let you know we are finished with the photo shoot. Unless you two need me for anything else, I'm going home and sleeping for the next twelve hours straight. I think I caught a cold in Vegas."

"You're lucky if that's all you caught," I tease.

"I didn't fuck anyone in Vegas but Jennifer," he says, offended.

"Are you and Jennifer okay?" Keatyn asks him.

"I'm pissed she texted her ex while she was with me. Makes sense now why she wouldn't sleep with Riley. I think she's still sort of hung up on him."

"I think her drunken mind thought she was getting back at him," Keatyn says. "She has a big crush on you, Knox. Go easy on her."

"I think it would be best if we were just friends going forward."

"Don't tell her that today, okay?" I tell him.

"I won't. I might not tell her for a while. She's fun. But I will probably have the *this is just fun* chat with her soon."

"I think she'll be okay with that," Keatyn says.

"You've been here all day," Knox says to Keatyn. "Don't you think you should go get some rest?"

"I was thinking the same thing," Aiden says, joining us all in the office.

"It's no wonder I can't get anything done," she teases. "It's like Grand Central Station in here!"

"You and Aiden head home," I tell her, exiting her office. "I think you've done everything you can for today. Dawson and I will go back over all the details and get ready for tomorrow."

I DECIDE TO stop freaking out about Dawson. Maybe I'm *feeling* in love with him or maybe I'm *really* in love with him. Either way, Keatyn's right. I should enjoy it while it lasts.

"Did you find what you were looking for?" Dawson asks when I sit down next to him in the board room.

"I think I found exactly what I've been looking for." I smile at him. I can't help it.

"Good. I've been running through our to-do list and went over it with Tyler. I think we've got everything covered for today." He stands up and rubs my shoulders. "You're tense."

"What would you think of getting a massage?" I ask him.

"I know I'd love to massage you."

"Are you good with your hands?"

He leans down and whispers in my ear. "I think you already know the answer to that question. Shall I give you a massage tonight?"

"Well, I was thinking of having Chad, my masseuse, give us both a massage."

"Oh," Dawson says flatly. "I should have known. The girl who has everything." He stops rubbing my neck. "I'm sorry. That came out wrong. Do you sleep with him? You were glad I didn't sleep with anyone in Vegas, but what about you? Are you seeing anyone?"

"No."

"Were you before I got here?"

"I didn't sit home alone, if that's what you mean," I reply brusquely, becoming a little offended.

"So where are these guys now?"

"It was casual."

"So just sex?"

"And the occasional escort to a party. Although, lately, I've been taking Chad. He loves parties and he's been meeting a lot of men that way."

"Men?"

"Yes, he's gay."

Dawson sits on the table in front of me and smiles.

"That makes you happy?" I ask.

"Yes," he says, brushing his lips across mine, his jealousy making me feel giddy.

"Let's skip the massage, go to the restaurant downstairs, and have some dinner."

"I'm making everyone stay until nine tonight. That's supposed to include us."

"Let them go home. Tomorrow is going to be busy when word of the party gets out."

"I don't know," I say, knowing I personally have yet to run through the list and verify that everything was done the way I wanted.

"I'll bring the list. We'll go over it while we enjoy a bottle of wine."

I move my head around, thinking about it, as he sweetens the deal. "Then I'll take you back to my place and massage every square inch of you."

"Deal," I say. How can I refuse? "But you have to promise that if there's something we missed on the list, we'll finish it before we leave."

"I promise," he says, sealing it with a kiss.

CAPTIVE FILMS—SANTA MONICA
KEATYN

AFTER EVERYONE BUT Aiden leaves, I tell him, "We're going to have to reschedule dinner with our families."

He hands me the frozen lemonade in his hand and gets a stubborn look on his face.

"No way, Boots. This is more important than *any* crisis. Besides, Tyler told me everything is under control."

"Tyler is an optimist."

Aiden pulls me up out of my chair and wraps his arms around me. I can't help but melt into him.

"You hired Vanessa to handle all this kind of stuff. Let her do her job."

"Hugging you takes away all my stress," I coo, sliding my hands up under his shirt.

"Don't start what you can't finish," he teases, giving me a steamy kiss.

I stifle a yawn.

"See, you're tired. You've already been at work for over twelve hours. It's time for us to go to dinner."

"The photographer is working overtime to get the photos from today's shoot back to me. Once I choose them, they have to go to the printer, who is working overnight to get the promotional posters for the party done."

"When will they be done?"

"He said around nine."

"Message him now to text you when they are done. We won't stay at dinner long and when we get home, I'll help you choose. I'm thinking a nice warm bath is in order too."

"Do I have to bathe alone?" I ask, moving my hand a little lower.

"Do you ever?" he teases, kissing my nose. "Come on, baby. Let's go share some good news."

AIDEN AND I are sitting in the bathtub. He's cupping water in his hand and emptying it on my chest to keep me warm while I'm leaned back against his chest, relaxing.

"Everyone was excited about the baby," he says, referring to the cheers and the, *It's about times* from our families.

"Your mom especially," I say. His mom fought and won a battle with cancer and is so excited to have lived to see this day.

"Your sisters are excited to become aunts, but I think they were even more excited to learn that the fundraiser invitations they got yesterday are really for our wedding."

"I know. Did you hear Avery asking about interning at Captive? She said her teacher won't count all the work she does on their Stevens brand."

"You were smart to tell her yes. Your marketing department can always use help in social media."

"I know. With Gracie's acting, Ivery's modeling, and Emery's music career, I think Avery sometimes feels like the oddball. She's yet to really find her calling."

"Your sisters are the exception. Most people don't know what they want to do until they experience life. Want to know what I think?"

"Of course."

"I think she could be a Captive Films executive someday. She's smart and creative."

"Aiden, ohmigosh, I never even thought of that, but you're right. I have a better idea. I should let her spend a few weeks in each department so she can figure out what she loves the most."

"That's perfect. Speaking of perfect. So far, Ariela seems to be doing a great job getting this wedding pulled together. I think we were smart to take a page from the Abby Johnston and Tommy Stevens handbook on how to quietly get married."

"I think so too. Maggie texted me and told me Ariela had meetings with vendors all day today. And she got the invitations out on time. Even I didn't know if that was possible."

My phone dings. Aiden wipes his hand off on a towel and looks at it. "Guess the bath party is over. That's the photographer. The photos are ready. Oh, there's also a text from Dallas. We must have not heard it when you were attacking me."

I laugh. "I'm pretty sure it's *you* who did the attacking this time. What's it say?"

"It says, *Call me.* Here, I'll dial. Your hands are wet."

He puts it on speaker.

"Hey, Dallas. It's me and Aiden. Sorry we just saw your text."

"How did dinner with the families go?"

"Good. Everyone is excited about both the wedding and the baby."

"I knew they would be. So, I may have some good news. I've been working on these charges with the county prosecutor. I told him in confidence about the publicity stunt."

"Oh, Dallas! That's brilliant. It's another way the press could verify it."

"That's what I was thinking. I believe they will be dropping all the charges except for the public intoxications and all that requires is paying a fine."

"You're amazing."

"The casino and hotel also called. Apparently, they have been flooded with calls inquiring about the suite from the party and have booked it out for months in advance. The crew is welcome back anytime."

"Don't tell them that," Aiden laughs.

CAPTIVE FILMS—SANTA MONICA
DAWSON

AFTER DINNER WE go back to the office to tie up a few final details.

"Will you be my date for the Purity Party? Apparently, Tyler ordered me an all-white suit. I haven't worn all white since my wedding," I accidentally say. Shit, I don't want to talk about my wedding.

"I told you about my wedding," Vanessa says. "What was yours like?"

"A bit of a disaster. Her family was embarrassed she was getting married after she had a baby and refused to come. My family didn't want me to marry her, but they came because we always support each other."

"She had a beautiful family with you. Why would she kill herself?"

"Because she was in a severe depression."

"Why?"

"I really don't want to talk about it, Vanessa. I told you she struggled with depression. I'm sorry I brought up my wedding. I didn't mean to."

"Oh," she says. "It's okay." But I can tell it's not really.

She's quiet for a minute then says, "So tomorrow night is the party. What do you want to do Friday night? I think if we're able to pull this all off, we should go out and celebrate."

"I can't on Friday night. The girls will be in town."

"We'll include them in the celebration."

"I think that I need to spend the weekend with them, uh, *alone*." I stress.

"Oh," she says again.

Then there's silence.

"We've been making plans all week for what they want to do when they get here. They deserve my full attention," I say, then trying to make it up to her, I slide my hand onto her thigh. "And you are a beautiful distraction."

She immediately stands up. "Well, since we're all fin-ished up here, I'm heading home. Thanks for all your help today, Dawson. I'll see you bright and early in the morning."

"You don't want to come back to my place for a massage?"

"No, I'm very tired. It's been a long day. Good night, Dawson," she says, then quickly walks out the door.

Shit.

RILEY'S PENTHOUSE — L.A.
RILEY

I'M SITTING ALONE in my penthouse staring out at the view, trying to avoid the phone in my lap.

After the photo shoot, Keatyn sent me home but asked me to keep my phone on. Thankfully, I was so tired I did nothing but shower and then fall on my bed and pass out.

But, now, the phone is taunting me.

I have twenty-four unread text messages, waiting to be read.

I have no idea who they are from, but I'm sure at least one is from Ariela.

I'm trying not to obsess over whether or not I should read them, but that's exactly what's on my mind.

Fuck it.

I know I probably shouldn't go out after everything that's happened, but I don't feel like being alone.

So I'm going to the bar for just one drink.

I'M AT THE bar for about ten minutes when I notice two young blondes staring at me, then talking about me, then looking at their phones to confirm what they thought; that I am indeed Riley Johnson.

I roll my eyes and look around the room, searching for

someone who might not know who I am. Who might not care what I could do for their career.

My mind flits back to Ariela holding her shoes and wrapped in her husband's arms.

Next thing I know, a high-pitched voice says boldly, "Buy me a drink?"

I turn, wondering if that line actually works for her. The girl has a fresh-faced Midwestern look set on the body of a porn star.

I'm thinking it does.

"Sure, why not?" I raise my finger in the air to summon the bartender. "Get this lady a drink."

She orders some sort of fruity concoction and quickly downs it.

Then she sets to work on me; touching my arm, giggling, leaning forward to allow me a closer look at her cleavage, which is prominently on display in a low-cut, skintight dress.

"You wanna get out of here?" I ask. I'm not in the mood for flirting. I'm in the mood for fucking.

"I thought you'd never ask."

When the valet pulls up in tonight's ride, you can practically see the dollar signs blazing in her eyes.

"Ohmigawd! You have a Poorsh," she exclaims, slaughtering the Porsche name.

ON THE SHORT drive to my penthouse, she gives me an excellent blowjob, which is always a sign of good things to come.

Pun intended.

Once she's naked on my bed, I reach into my nightstand and pull out a couple silk scarves. This chick looks a little like Shelby, and I'm thinking she may have the same taste in sex.

"I'm going to tie you up," I tell her.

Her eyes get big but then she quickly purrs, "Of course. Whatever you want."

Once she's pinned to my bed, I position myself above her.

But the closer I get to her the more scared she looks.

Is she afraid?

Of me?

I study her more closely, realizing she looks pretty young. But she had to be twenty-one to be at the bar.

I think back to my college days and the fake IDs we all had.

"How old are you?"

"Twenty," she says, but she's not a good actress.

"How old are you really?" I ask sternly.

"Um, nineteen."

"And how long have you been in L.A.?"

"A year."

"And why are you here with me?"

"Because you're hot," she says, trying to convince me, but not succeeding.

I frown and shake my head, suddenly pissed.

"Don't lie to me! Why are you here? Why did you come home with me when you don't even know me?"

She doesn't bother trying to act this time, but she still lies. "Your name doesn't matter, baby. I think you're sexy."

I get in her face. "Tell me the fucking truth."

She sighs, her perky breasts rising and falling. "Fine. Because you're Riley Johnson."

I sit on top of her, grab a pocketknife from my bedside

table, and flip open the blade.

Her eyes get huge and she starts to cry. "What . . . What are you gonna do with the knife?"

I quickly cut the ties, jump off her, and pull on my pants. My boner is long gone.

"Get out of here," I command.

She sits up.

"Wait! It's fine. I'm kinky. I love that stuff. I was just acting. Pretending to be inexperienced. I'd be perfect for the role of Miranda in the new teen romance you're casting."

I narrow my eyes at her.

"Get the fuck out of here. And for the record, serious actresses don't have to sleep with the producer to get a role. They're good actresses. I have never and *will never* hire a girl who acts like a whore."

"Word about that gets out and you'll never get a date," she mutters as she's pulling on her dress.

I take two steps toward her and grab her by the arm. "What the fuck did you say?"

She glares at me. "I'm sure you heard *exactly* what I said. Are you stupid? Why else would I want to sleep with some old guy? I'm just tired of getting nowhere."

She grabs her purse and storms out of the bedroom in tears.

I follow her toward my elevator, push the button, and don't give a shit about how she gets home.

Fuck.

I plop down on my hard, modern leather sofa. Then quickly get back up and stare down at what the interior designer called *a statement piece*.

I look around at my penthouse. Dark woods, sleek furniture, lots of metal and leather.

It's like the inside of a fucking car, not a home.

I grab my phone and call Aiden.

Keatyn answers. "Riley, this better not be your one call from jail."

I glance at the modern clock above my fireplace, realizing how late it is.

"It's not. Sorry, I know it's late. Fuck. Can I come over? I need to talk to Aiden."

"Of course you can, Riley. Are you okay?"

"Not really," I say and hang up.

I hit an app on my phone to get a black car. I'm not in the mood to drive.

ON THE WAY to Malibu, I wonder what in the hell I'm even going to say to Aiden. Truth is, I needed to get out of my cold penthouse.

I have the driver drop me off at the public beach.

I take my shoes off and walk in the sand, then sneak under the chain link fence into the Malibu Colony. I look up at the moon, thankful for the light.

I close my eyes and take a deep breath, then make my way up their deck and knock on the window.

Aiden comes to the door wearing just shorts.

"Is that what you wear to bed?" I ask as he lets me in.

"Did you come out here at two in the morning to ask me that?" he chuckles.

"No. Where's Keatyn?"

"I told her to go back to sleep."

"She gonna listen to you?"

He laughs. "Probably not. So, what's going on?"

"A girl I brought home tonight called me an old guy. When did we become old guys?"

"Well, I am almost thirty."

"Fine. *You're* an old guy. I'm still twenty-eight for a few more days. Do I look old?"

"You look successful, Riley," Keatyn says, walking into the study wearing a short silk robe and carrying a tray of warm, fresh-from-the-oven chocolate chip cookies and three tall glasses of milk.

"I'm gonna defer to her on that," Aiden says. "No offense, but I don't really pay attention to how you look."

Keatyn hands me a plate with four cookies and I take a glass of milk off the tray. When I got here, I wanted a scotch, but this is even better.

As I bite into the gooey cookie, I survey their home, wondering why it's one of my favorite places. The walls are the color of sand. There's a worn leather chair in the corner and photos on the shelves. It smells clean like the ocean. And I realize it reminds me of our place in the Hamptons, where I'm surrounded by family.

And that's how I feel here; like I'm surrounded by family.

"These are good," I tell her. "Thanks."

She's perched on the edge of Aiden's chair. One of his hands is protectively wrapped around her side and the other is bringing a cookie to his mouth.

Me, I'm double fisting it; cookie in one hand, milk in the other.

Bite. Drink. Repeat.

Keatyn gets up and gives Aiden a kiss. "I'll let you boys talk." On the way out of the room, she kisses the top of my head. "If you dated girls your own age, Riley, you wouldn't feel old."

"How does she always know what's wrong before I even

say it?" I ask Aiden, who's now double fisting milk and cookies too.

"Is that really why you're here? Because a girl called you old?"

"That's part of it."

"It's Ariela, isn't it?"

"It's all of it. I'm tired of fucking a different girl every night. It's exhausting. My penthouse feels cold. I have so much stuff—"

"And no one to share it with?" he says, finishing my sentence.

"Yeah."

"And the girl you want to share it with broke your heart. Twice now."

"Yeah."

"Riley, what do they say about Captive Films? About you?"

I chuckle. "That I'm the king of romance. Ironic, huh? I haven't romanced a girl since her."

"What's the one thing about romance? About love?"

"It's a risk. If I could just get inside her head and know what she's thinking. It's funny, really. You know how Keatyn turned her journals into the screenplays and now the books. She was telling me the other day that readers are clamoring for a book from your point of view."

"You know she won't allow that. She says it would ruin the story."

"Exactly. If the audience would've known what you were thinking, there wouldn't have been any drama or mystery."

"And they'd be pissed to know that although I did totally fall in love with her that day, I still mostly wanted to sleep with her. I thought after my prom gone bad that I had grown up and was different, but I still had a lot of growing up to do. We both did. I was crazy about her but there were times when I wanted to give up. Times when I thought we'd never make it. Love requires work, Riley. It's risking your heart. It's wooing her when she has a boyfriend or is still seeing her ex. You and Ariela never had much drama. Once you asked her out, you never really broke up. I mean, until that day."

"Graduation day," I say, taking a gulp of milk and shoving another cookie into my mouth.

"Riley, did you fight for her?"

I hang my head. "I was too devastated to fight. Then I was pissed. Then it was too late."

"She's back. You have a chance. Why don't you stop fucking around and take it?"

"If she—"

"If she breaks your heart, we'll deal with it," he tells me. "Call her and find out what really happened."

"What do you mean? I know what happened."

"Riley, you're trying to fuck your feelings away. It's not going to work. And what do you know exactly?"

"I don't care what Vanessa says. I know what I saw."

"Yeah, you saw her husband kiss her."

"That was enough."

"Did you bother to ask him *why* he kissed her?"

"No! Why the fuck would I do that? It's her fucking husband."

"You did once before. Don't you remember?"

"What do you mean?" I ask, bewildered.

"Remember Christmas break senior year? You were at Ariela's house and some guy dropped by."

"Yeah, her idiot ex-boyfriend. He tried to kiss her and I whooped his ass."

"So, why didn't you whoop Collin's ass this time?"

"Wait? What the fuck? Are you telling me that's who she married?"

"Yeah."

"But he was such a douche!"

"Still is, from what I gather. Riley, if you're going to have a relationship with Ariela, you have to talk to her. You have to believe her when she tells you what happened. The Riley I know would have seen him kiss her, walked straight up to him, knocked him the fuck out, and—"

"—asked questions later," I say along with him. I take another cookie. "You're right. I've become a pussy."

Aiden laughs. "You haven't become a pussy. You can't knock someone out in business when things don't go your way. I'd say you're more refined. But you haven't been in love for a while. You're out of practice."

"It always seems so easy for you and Keatyn."

"It's not. We make it work because we want it to work. Our relationship has always been our number one priority. You know how many roles she's turned down because of scheduling. Riley, I'm going to ask you one question. It's the only question that really matters. Do you still love Ariela?"

I slowly nod.

"Then go fucking do something about it and don't let anything get in the way."

"Now?"

"Yes, now."

"I can't."

"Why not?"

"I think Keatyn and Dallas are right. I need to go back

to Eastbrooke and put the past behind me before I can move on."

"Does that mean you're going?"

"Yeah, I am."

"Then congratulations are in order too. Riley Johnson CEO & Chairman of the Board has a nice ring to it."

"I was so shocked, I never asked her why she was promoting me."

Keatyn walks out with another plate of cookies and sets them on the table. "Why don't you just stay here tonight, Riley." It's hard to even look at her. I'm so overcome with emotion. I'm so lucky to have such good friends. "I'm promoting you for a lot of reasons but mostly because you deserve it."

"Is one of the reasons because you want to slow down?"

"We want to spend more time at the vineyard," Aiden says. "Raise our family there."

"That sounds nice," I say.

"I want to take some time off and just write scripts for a while. It's what I love. And I want that for you too, Riley," Keatyn tells me. "Dallas has always been so good about having balance between his personal and professional life. You and I need to do a better job of it. That's part of why I brought Dawson in. I want you to groom him to be your successor. Once you feel he's ready to take over as CEO, you'll retain the Chairman of the Board title and only have to attend board meetings."

"It would be cool to only work on the fun projects. I've been sorta itching to produce again. Be on set more often."

"It's not like you even need to work anymore, Riley. You have plenty of money. You should be doing what you love."

"And finding love?" I say with a smirk, knowing where the conversation is headed.

"At least having *the time* for love," she replies.

Thursday, October 9th

CAPTIVE FILMS—SANTA MONICA
VANESSA

THE PURITY PARTY invitations have been delivered, the event is being set up, and I'm leaning back in Keatyn's office chair taking a breather when Avery steps in. She started work today as a Captive Films intern and jumped straight into the fire.

"So, I will admit, I follow most of the big tabloids," she says. "Something just got posted that you should see."

"Is it good or bad?"

"I know how good my sister is at handling the press. She says she learned from our mom and Knox. I showed this to a couple people in the marketing department and they were shocked, which means my sister, and probably you, planned it that way. My guess is the Vegas thing was as bad as it seemed, and you two turned it around to make it look like a publicity stunt. Am I right?"

"Close the door," I tell her. "Have you told anyone else your thoughts?"

"No. If I'm right, we wouldn't want anyone to know."

I nod my head at her. "You're very astute for someone your age, Avery."

She does a little clap. "I knew I was right!"

"Are you having fun today?"

"Actually, yes. I kind of thought working here might be corporate and boring, but it's not. Everyone is cool."

"Keatyn told me she wants you to try your hand at the different divisions of the company, but what's your passion?"

She looks at her feet.

"What?" I say. "You can tell me."

"I know the tabloids say things to sell papers. I know some of the things they print are lies set in a teeny bit of truth. I know some are boldfaced lies. But it's exciting, don't you think? The way people are perceived in public. The face they choose to show. The trouble they get into. How it can be manipulated."

"Sounds like you'd be good at public relations. You ever want to work directly with me, you let me know."

"Really? Ohmigawd," she says, sounding just like Keatyn. "I would totally love that!"

"Good. Now, are you going to tell me what the article says?"

"Ohmigosh, I almost forgot! Let me read it to you! It says . . .

The Golden Ticket

Well, people.

I'm holding in my hand a gorgeous white glittery invitation on paper so thick you could sleep on it. Captive Films invited yours truly to what they are calling a Purity Party to promote a new film project.

Attendees have been asked to wear—you guessed it—white.

Included with the invitation is a glossy photo of Jennifer Edwards wearing a skimpy white lingerie angel costume—complete with feather wings—and tossing away a halo. On the edge of the photo, there are two sets of male hands waiting to catch it. The bottom simply says #DaddysAngel.

After scouring the internet for information about this project, I came up empty. So I decided to do it the old-fashioned way. I hit up my sources inside the film company.

And here's what I learned:

Jennifer Edwards, Knox Daniels, and Jake Worth will be starring in Daddy's Angel. *No word on what the movie is about, other than Jennifer's role will showcase a double life. Her minister father thinks she's still a virgin, when in truth, she's promiscuous, wild, and a bit of a hellcat. Rumor also has it that Captive Films' CEO, Riley Johnson, will have a cameo role.*

So here's the deal. This party has me wondering. Was the group's recent crazy Vegas weekend—which landed them all in jail—just a publicity stunt?

Now I'm off to buy something white and fabulous to wear tonight. Who cares that it's after Labor Day. When you're as successful as Captive Films, you can break the rules.

Also, did you notice the unnamed hottie in the Vegas photos? My sources say that it is none other than Riley's brother, Dawson Johnson, a recent addition to the Captive Films executive team.

P.S. Watch out Hemsworths, your reign as the world's hottest brothers may be coming to an end.

P.P.S. Speaking of watching out . . . Dawson, I'll be stalking you tonight. I'll be the one in . . . Well, white.

"That's just great," I mutter, feeling jealous at the mention of Dawson.

"So this article could be just the beginning," Avery says, reminding me that she's still sitting in front of me. "Don't you think since she suggested it, everyone will believe it?"

"That's what we're hoping for. Are you coming to the party tonight?"

"Yes, Mom's letting me borrow a gorgeous white dress. She hasn't even worn it yet. I'm so excited!"

"Why don't you hang out near the door with Tyler and greet people."

"Really? Ohmigawd, that would be amazing! Thanks, Vanessa. I'm heading home now to get ready."

"Have fun. I'll tell Tyler and see you tonight."

"Did you get a dress?"

"I haven't had time. I have some white dresses at home that will work," I say.

"I thought you might say that," she says, running out of the room and returning with a long dress bag. "I brought a dress for you to wear."

"You did?"

"Yes, it was one of the dresses Mom had. You know designers are always sending her things. I saw the dress and knew it would look perfect on you. Or at least the you that you are today."

"What do you mean?"

"You seem different. Happier than I've seen you in a while. This is a happy dress."

"A happy dress?"

"It's hard to explain, but yes. If you end up not liking it, it's okay. I won't be offended. I'll see you tonight!"

After she leaves, I think about two things. About the reporter who will be stalking Dawson at the party, and that except for today, Avery is right, I have been the happiest I've been in a while.

Because of Dawson.

I acted like a little jealous brat last night and have been avoiding him all day.

And I understand. I do.

But it still hurt.

And the hurt surprised me.

And that made me mad.

At myself.

I look at the clock. Three hours until party time.

But I have one more thing to take care of before I go get ready.

ASHER VINEYARDS—SONOMA COUNTY
ARIELA

I'M JUST WALKING back into Maggie's office after my visit to the bakery to finalize the wedding cake details when I get a call from Collin.

"Your dad told me the good news."

"I told him the good news on Tuesday. I expected to hear from you sooner."

"I was out of the office until today."

"What were you doing?"

"I took a couple personal days, Ariela," he spews. "My wife filed for divorce. It kinda shook me."

"Sure it did. You were so shook up that you went straight to your secretary's arms."

"Are you having me followed?"

"Actually, yes. And I have pictures."

"Pictures of what?"

"Of you boning your secretary, *darling*."

"You're lying, pumpkin. You would never think to do something like that. You trust me. You're just testing me."

"Trust me, pumpkin. I'm not lying. I'm also working on a special surprise for you."

"Yeah, your dad told me. You're throwing a holiday party for all my clients. Big whoop."

"That was supposed to be a secret."

"Your dad and I are tight."

"Collin, a quick uncontested divorce from your boss' daughter that is nice and clean and agreeable, will be much better for you than one where all your dirty laundry gets aired by your wife."

"You would look like a fool. No way you'd do that to your dad. You don't have the balls."

"I've grown a big set of balls in the last couple of weeks, Collin. Trust me, I already have the invitations being printed."

"Big deal. Who you gonna send them to?"

"I take it my dad didn't tell you everything. Like the fact that he gave me your entire client list?"

"Uh, no."

"See, here's the thing, Collin. I flat out lied to my dad. Wanna know what I'm really going to send out?"

"What?"

"Gorgeous Thanksgiving cards featuring two photos. One from our beautiful wedding and another of you breaking your vows by screwing your secretary in her living room."

"You wouldn't."

"Oh, yes. I would. In fact, if you contest the divorce, that's exactly what I'll do."

"I'll take my chances. Most of the men I know would applaud me. My secretary is smoking hot."

"You're right. They might. Fortunately for me, most of them are married to women who don't work. Women who get the mail. Women who would be upset by what they saw. You wanted to pretend we have an amazing, stable marriage. You wanted me to have the perfect car, the perfect handbag, the perfect house. Appearances are everything to you and your business."

"Whatever."

"Collin, you don't work very hard because my dad gives you all his new business. If these photos go out, it will hurt my dad's business. Do you really think your pretty partnership will happen after that?"

"Uh . . ."

"Exactly. Oh, hang on. Let me send you a mock-up of the card I sent to the printers. It's cute. There's even a poem. You'll get a kick out of it."

"I don't believe you."

"Believe it, Collin. I'm hanging up now. Enjoy your card."

I'M SHAKING AGAIN when I hang up.

"I didn't mean to eavesdrop," Maggie says, "But fuck

yeah! I'm so proud of you for standing up to that asshole!"
She studies me. "You know what. You look like you could
use a glass of wine. Fortunately, that's something we have
plenty of here. Red or white?"

"White. I can't believe I said all that. My dad is going to
be mad at me when he finds out I lied to him."

"And do you care about that?" she asks as she drags me
out of her office, across the street to her house, and onto her
front porch. "Sit and rock. I'll be right back."

I sit down and rock. And rock.

And feel a little calmer.

By the time she comes back with two glasses of a crisp
Chardonnay, I say, "I'm proud of me too."

"You should be. Can I see the Thanksgiving card?"

"Sure." I hand her my phone.

"Oh, wow. You even made up a little rhyme.

We should thank you for your business this
Thanksgiving day,
But, instead, we find Collin and his secretary rolling in
the hay.
Yes, he has a wife who you all know,
But does that really matter?
Boys will be boys and all that chatter.
If you're a wife and know how I feel,
Show Collin you won't stand for this deal.
Move your business to someone worthy of your trust.
And not someone who just thinks about lust.
Maybe it's time us women unite.
Like the Pilgrims and Indians did that night.
So Happy Thanksgiving,

enjoy your cranberry sauce
And know I'm divorcing this asshole,
Love, Ariela Ross."

"What do you think?"

"I think if you stop planning weddings, you could write divorce cards. It's awesome. Are you really going to send them?"

"It all depends on if Collin decides to play nice."

"If I saw this, I'd be playing nice. So how is the wedding planning going?"

"Good. Your vendors are all super nice and more than willing to go out of their way to get this *fundraiser* done in time. The only thing I'm worried about is having them set up the furniture for the ceremony. The altar will scream wedding."

"They deliver it the afternoon of the wedding, right?"

"Yeah."

"Well, worse case, we say that Logan and I are renewing our vows."

"Oh, that's good."

"Logan has a dinner to attend tonight. Maybe we could have a girls' night. Order some gourmet pizza, get drunk on wine, and catch up."

"That sounds perfect."

CAPTIVE FILMS—SANTA MONICA
DAWSON

"YOU'VE BEEN AVOIDING me all day," I say to Vanessa as I join her in Keatyn's office.

"I'm not avoiding you. I'm just busy."

"Vanessa, don't shut me out."

I look at him and sigh. "Avery gave me a happy dress to wear tonight."

"A happy dress?"

"Yes, she says I've been happy lately. I have been because of you. I'm sorry I got upset last night. I was mad at myself, not mad at you."

I shut the door. "Why were you mad at yourself?"

"Because I wanted to be included. I understand completely why you need to spend time alone with your girls, I do. But my first reaction was that I was jealous. I was mad at myself for behaving that way. I just couldn't help it."

"You're lucky Keatyn's office is full of windows," I say.

"Stop grinning," she says, giving me a swat. "And stop with the sexy eyes."

"I have sexy eyes?"

"You know damn well you do. Do you want to stay here while I make a call? Might as well learn more about what I do. It's not always pretty."

"What are you gonna do?" I ask.

"A little PR blackmail."

"Interesting." I take off my jacket, lay it on the couch, and then roll up my sleeves.

"Now, you're stripping?"

"Just getting comfortable."

Tyler knocks on the door, interrupting us. "I just got a call from a tabloid that I 'leak' things to on occasion. She said that Knox's assistant told her *off the record* that Vegas was a publicity stunt and that someone, who would surprise us, leaked the photos."

"What did you tell her?"

"Well, you told us to say no comment so I said *no comment.*"

"Perfect. I'm just getting ready to call that someone and persuade him to confess that he pushed out the photos."

"Oh, how are you going to do that?"

Vanessa tosses a photo in Tyler's direction. He catches it out of the air.

"Oh, my stars! Parker Hudson?" He holds the photo up to the light. "Where the hell was this party and why wasn't I invited?"

Vanessa laughs. "Show Dawson."

He hands it to me. My eyes get big. "Jeez. You could have warned me." I turn the paper on it's side and tilt my head. "Wow."

"It all works just fine, Mr. Johnson," Tyler teases. "I know these things."

"I'm sure it does. But I'd prefer not to see it."

"Well, here's hoping that Parker prefers everyone not see it. Hush, you both, I'm going to call him."

Tyler sits next to me on the couch in rapture. If I didn't know he was gay, I'd think he had a crush on Vanessa.

"Isn't she just amazing?" he says to me. "Did you see her handbag today? Brand new. I heard there's a wait list. She's always one of the first ones they call. Lucky bitch."

I chuckle, but Vanessa shushes me. It's kinda hot.

Kinda like being scolded by your hot teacher.

My mind starts wandering as she puts the call on speaker and says, "Parker, how are you? Thanks for agreeing to chat with me."

"My publicist made me," he says.

"Well, he's smart because we have some publicity to talk about. I'm just gonna cut to the chase, Parker. I know that you sold the photos of Vegas to the tabloids. Jennifer was supposedly drunk and you thought she was trying to make you jealous. I'd even bet a lot of money that new girlfriend of yours—the playboy bunny—whatever her name is, encouraged you to sell them."

"Uh," he stutters.

"You don't have to answer, Parker. It's okay. So you sold the photos. The press ate them up. You made a tidy sum that, you will be announcing today, will be donated to Jennifer's favorite charity."

"The fuck I am. I didn't sell anything."

"Parker, Jennifer texted you sixty-one photos. All of which have been sold to the press. You tried to split them up, but I know people and they told us that it was you. Makes sense, as no one else would have a selfie that Jennifer took herself. Now, I know you are hot. Your fans love you. But recently, I received just one photo of you. A photo of you so damning, you'll be swimming in a shit sewer of bad PR from which your career will never recover."

"Bullshit."

"Hang on, Parker. I'm going to use my cell phone to text you the photo."

She obviously had it pre-loaded into her phone, because all she does is hit send.

"I just heard your phone vibrate. You must have gotten it already. Amazing how fast photos can travel nowadays, isn't it? I wonder what would happen if all the mothers of your teenybopper fans caught wind of this."

"Oh, fuck," Parker says.

"The perfect comment," Vanessa continues. "Now that I have your attention. What are you going to do tonight?"

"Announce that I sold the photos because I'm an asshole. That I'll be donating the proceeds to the children's foundation she supports. She did it on purpose, didn't she? She knew that I would do it. She was just pretending to be drunk. I heard it was a publicity stunt."

"I have no comment on that, but I do have another comment. I'd like you to do a few interviews with the press. I'd like you to publicly apologize to Jennifer for being the douche that you are. Never once did she come out and tell anyone why she broke up with you. She never told them you were a lying cheater. She has class. It's time for you to tell the truth."

"I can't do that."

"Oh. I see. Okay. Well, nice chatting with you. Um, you might want to notify your PR firm about what's coming up. You know, so they can prepare."

"Fuck. Fine. Fine. I'll do it."

"And you'll dump the bunny. She isn't good for you."

"Yes, yes. I'll do it."

"Perfect. Then it will stay between you and me. Cheers, Parker. Have a great night!"

She hangs up and Tyler stands up and claps. "I want to be you when I grow up. Spectacular performance. Now, you need to get going, or you will be late for your appointments. And by the way, I saw the dress Avery brought you, To. DIE. For. See you tonight."

He rushes out of the door, already on his phone.

I saunter over to Vanessa and sit on the edge of the desk next to her. "If Tyler's gonna die, that means your dress is probably going to make me hot."

"I haven't even seen it yet. It may not even fit me."

"Uh, huh."

"Fine. I peeked. It's gorgeous. I'm hoping I can do it

justice."

"Wear your red lipstick. I'll pick you up at seven."

"Six-thirty. I need to be there early."

I lean in and kiss her. "You really are amazing."

ASHER VINEYARDS—SONOMA COUNTY
ARIELA

I HAD SO much fun catching up and reminiscing, and maybe getting a little drunk, with Maggie tonight. As I plop down on the bed and am trying, unsuccessfully, to get my boots off, my phone dings.

I fall off the bed trying to get it, hoping it's Riley.

Coffee Kyle: *So did you go? Did you see him? Is there a sweet job waiting for me?*

Me: *Yes. Yes. Unfortunately not.*

Coffee Kyle: *So what happened when you saw him?*

Me: *The first time he saw me, he was pissed I was there but gave me the hottest kiss.*

Coffee Kyle: *Mine would have been hotter.*

Me: *Don't mess with me. I'm a little drunk. And there was a lot of emotion in this kiss.*

Coffee Kyle: *I'm just teasing. So a kiss. Then did you have hot angry sex?*

Me: *I wish. No.*

Coffee Kyle: *Come on, give me the scoop. I sat through a six-hour movie with you. I need to know the rest of the story.*

Me: *I don't think this story is going to have a happy ending, Kyle. It's all kind of a mess.*

Coffee Kyle: *So, truth. I saw the Vegas photos. That's really what made me text you. How are you doing?*

Me: *I'm a bit of a wreck but I'm busy. I got a job running a big swanky event. You know what? I could really use some help. Would you want to be my assistant?*

Coffee Kyle: *Do I get to ass—ist you in the bedroom?*

Me: *No, but I'll pay well.*

Coffee Kyle: *Sounds like I'm packing my bags now.*

Me: *Fly into San Francisco. The event is at a vineyard in Sonoma County.*

Coffee Kyle: *Are you being serious? You said you were drunkish.*

Me: *I'm serious.*

Coffee Kyle: *I'm-hanging-up-my-apron-and-telling-them-I-quit kind of serious?*

Me: *Why don't you hang up your apron, tell them you need a two week leave of absence, and see if you even like it here.*

Coffee Kyle: *You're awesome :) I'll be there Monday.*

Friday, October 10th

VANESSA'S ESTATE – HOLMBY HILLS
VANESSA

I WAKE UP, grab my phone off my nightstand, and see a text from Tyler with a link to an article about last night's party.

The Golden Ticket: Part Deaux.

Rumors are floating around that it was none other than Jennifer's ex, rocker Parker Hudson, who sold photos of the night in Vegas to the press.

When I asked Jennifer about it at the Purity Party, the actress, who sipped on sparkling Voss water all night, said Parker behaved exactly as expected.

For those of you who don't speak polite snark, she was saying that he was an ass and she fully expected him to do exactly what he did.

I'd say that pretty much confirms that even though Jennifer's stripper meme will live on forever, she's embracing it as part of this new role.

We're told the movie has been fast tracked and

that pre-production has already begun.

And now what you've been waiting for, the skinny on the party:

Jennifer looked amazing in a slinky red slip dress and white faux fur wrap. She was escorted into the party by not one, not two, not three, but four hot men. All in black. Jake Worth, who usually plays the perfect prince, shocked the hell out of us in his black Burberry motorcycle jacket, white henley, and black skinny jeans. We hear he's going to play the bad boy. Sa-wooon.

Guy number two was Knox Daniels looking delectable in a perfectly cut black-on-black Prada suit. Yum. He arrived with none other than Keatyn Douglas. I never get tired of seeing the pair together. And although Keatyn was showing off her massive engagement ring, it's pretty obvious, based on how close she stayed to Knox all night, that she and the winemaker will never make it down the aisle. She looked gorgeous, as usual, in a white jacquard Herve Leger bandage dress. But I'd like to be the first to go on record and say I've seen the girls in person and they have definitely been, shall we say, enhanced.

Guy number three was Captive Films CEO, Riley Johnson. Rather than wearing his usual suit and tie, Riley was in character as a sleazy photographer and dressed in a black velvet tuxedo. (Point to their stylist for that one.)

Guy number four was on my hit list. Riley's sexy brother and new man in town, Dawson Johnson. Dawson was wearing a black three-piece suit with a chambray oxford and matching hankie square. While I tried my best to hunt him down, he was busy chasing after publicist Vanessa Flanning. In the dress she was wearing, I can understand why.

P.S. On a side note, greeting us at the door was Avery Stevens, oldest daughter of Tommy Stevens and Abby Johnston. She was looking adorably angelic in a Marchesa baby doll dress. No word on if she'll have a role in Daddy's Angel.

I look at another text. This one from Jennifer.

Jennifer: I fired my publicist first thing this morning. I hope you will take me on as a client.

Me: It would be my pleasure. Can you meet for lunch today to discuss?

Jennifer: Sounds great. Thank you.

Another text pops up.

Dawson: Did you see the article? We did good! And, just for the record, she was right. I was chasing after you. Although you apologized in the office, you still seemed sorta mad last night . . . Are you?

Am I still mad at him?

No.

Do I understand his wanting to spend time alone with his daughters?

Yes.

Am I still hurt?

Yes.

Does that piss me off?

Yes.

Me: You're right. We did good. I won't be at Captive today. Have some other clients I need to deal with. I'll see you Monday. Have a good weekend with your girls.

God, I'm such a bitch.
I wait for him to reply.
But he doesn't.
And, honestly, I don't blame him.

TRINITY MOVIE SET — STUDIO CITY
KEATYN

"THIS WEEKEND IS gonna suck," Knox says, plopping down in my dressing room.

"Not for me. I got the weekend off," I say with a grin.

"Does that mean I'm off too?"

"Nope. They still want you in, but we did so well on our sex scenes we're a few days ahead of schedule."

"And then you're getting married. Where are you going on your honeymoon?"

"I'm not sure. Aiden is planning it. Somewhere remote and tropical, I hope."

"You'll need the rest because as soon as you get back, it's off on our whirlwind of locations."

"London, Paris, Prague, Dubai, and then New York. Then we're done with *Trinity* forever."

"Did you know they're talking about doing another one with the next generation? *Our* baby. Can you imagine? Promise me, no cameos unless we do them together."

"Oh wow. I hadn't heard that. But speaking of doing

something together, I read your script."

"And?"

"I'd love to do it with you if we could make a few tweaks."

"What kind of tweaks?"

"Well, you have it set in New York. Was there a specific reason for that?"

"Uh, not really."

"What if he meets her speed dating in San Francisco? Still a big city. And what if she works at a vineyard?"

"Are you suggesting we film it at your place?"

"Sort of. The people who own the land that butts up to ours are retiring and moving to Palm Springs. They asked Aiden if he'd be interested in buying their land. They plan to parcel it off and then sell their two houses separately. One is a quaint bed and breakfast that could be an adorable set. Near it are two very new and very large aluminum outbuildings. Much like the ones we're filming in now."

"Hmm. I like the idea. It'd certainly make for an easy commute for you."

"Knox, at one point, you were talking about buying a place out there. A getaway. The other home is a beautiful Tuscan-style villa set on the top of a hill. It has a similar view to ours, all the way to the ocean. A sweet infinity pool. I think you'd love it." I grin at him. "It'd make for an easy commute for you too."

"Are you suggesting I buy it and we fund this project ourselves?"

"Yeah, I am. We can always do a deal later with Captive for distribution."

"We'd stand to make more that way, wouldn't we?"

"If it performed well, yes. If not, we could lose a lot."

"For sure. Okay. Wow. You've given me a lot to think about. Something about finishing *Trinity* makes me feel like a grown up now. Does that even make sense?"

"It does," I say sadly, sitting down next to him and handing him an apple. "I sort of feel that way too. Like we're graduating."

"Yeah, that's it. We're graduating. On to the next great thing. And don't worry, sugar, I'll never forget that I was your first. It seems like yesterday."

"You're goofy. But you're right. You were my *first* screen test." I laugh at him. "It's amazing that we're even friends. You were such a jerk to me."

"Naw, I just played a jerk."

I give him a hug. He's going to make me start crying with all this nostalgia, so I change the subject. "So, what does grown up Knox want to do with his life?"

"Truth?"

"Yes."

"Don't tell anyone, but I'd like to get married and start a family. We've both put our lives on hold for these movies. Me more so than you."

"Are you thinking of settling down with Jennifer?"

"Uh, no. Maybe I could meet a cute little wine wench?"

"I don't even know what that is."

"Me either. I've never dated a normal girl."

"You have dated your fair share of crazies."

He swats me on the shoulder. "I meant normal as in not in the industry, not that they were crazy. I'm talking no models. No actresses. And definitely no makeup artists from the movie set. I will never date one of those again. What a flipping disaster that was. Part of me can't wait for this movie to be over, just so I won't have to look at her lying, cheating face every time I need powdered." He gives me a smirk. "You know what, you might be right. She was crazy. I mean, who in their fucking right mind would cheat on Knox "The Sexiest Man Alive" Daniels?"

"No one, Knox." I laugh. "No one. You know what? There are some normal people coming to the wedding. Quite a few of the women do work in the wine industry, although I would avoid the term *wine wench.*"

"I'm supposed to go to the wedding with Jennifer."

"Have you had the talk yet?"

"No. I was going to last night, but after the Parker Hudson interview, she was so damn happy I couldn't. Speaking of that, did you and Vanessa have anything to do with his sudden change of heart?"

I pull up a photo and show him my phone.

"Holy shit," he says, as he turns the phone sideways and starts blowing it up. "Shouldn't have done that." He laughs and covers his eyes. "Where did you get this?"

"I have good friends."

"Sander?"

"He is one such good friend."

"I can't believe you used to date him."

"Are you kidding me? He was the perfect boyfriend; he loved to shop, knew designer labels better than I did, and never, ever looked at other women."

"Fuck. You probably did love that. So it all makes sense now." He kisses my cheek and looks at the photo again. "I'm sure glad we're on the same side, sugar."

DAWSON'S BEACH HOUSE — MALIBU
DAWSON

I TWIRL HARLOW around on the beach then drop her into the sand as Ava skips through the water.

"What would you think about going over to the Santa Monica pier tonight? They have a Ferris wheel and music and lots of fun places to have dinner."

"Is Vanessa coming with us?" Harlow asks as we walk back toward the house.

"No. I thought you'd want to be alone with Daddy. Just the three of us."

"We think it would be more fun if she came with us," Ava agrees. The girls stand next to each other, arm in arm, smiling up at me.

"Well, since it's a rarity that you both agree on something, I guess I should give her a call." As I grab my phone off the stairs, I catch them high-fiving each other behind my back.

"What was that all about?" I ask, crossing my arms in front of me and giving them my sternest look.

"Um, nothing," Ava says, unconvincingly.

"Girls, don't lie to me."

"Uncle Cam promised us money if we could get you to spend time with her," Harlow admits.

"How much?"

"Twenty dollars," Ava says softly.

"Each!" Harlow exclaims, only to be punched in the arm by her sister.

"You can never keep a secret," Ava says to her.

"Tell you what," I say, stepping between them. "I'll give

you each twenty dollars right now if you'll sit down and talk to me honestly about Vanessa. Do you really want her to come with us?"

Ava grabs my hand and pulls me down on the step next to her. "It's okay with us if you have a girlfriend."

"Yeah, you're not getting any younger, Daddy," Harlow says, plopping down on my lap.

"And she's really pretty," Ava adds.

"And nice," Harlow says. "She rubbed my face while that silly Knox told us a bedtime story. And Grandma says you are getting old. And someday we will go off to college and you will be alone. We don't want you to be lonely, Daddy."

"I was married to your mom for a long time. And I didn't know how you would feel about me dating someone."

"It's okay, Daddy," Harlow says. "Mommy is in heaven. God is her boyfriend now."

"I think she'd date Jesus. He's younger." Ava says.

"Yes, Jesus," Harlow agrees. "Mama and Jesus. But Mama would make him shave his beard."

I laugh loudly envisioning Whitney ordering Jesus around.

"You two are silly," I say, tickling them.

"Daddy," Ava says seriously, "it's been two years since Mama died. Uncle Cam says if you don't use it—it will fall off and die. I'm pretty sure he was talking about your heart. Everyone needs someone to love."

"And me and my friend saw this movie where a dolphin was separated from her boyfriend and she wouldn't swim anymore," Harlow says dramatically. "And it was *so* sad. Her poor little heart just withered up and died! We don't want your heart to die or fall off!"

"Well, I certainly don't want that either."

"Then call her!"

I hit Vanessa's number but it goes to her voicemail. "Hey, it's me. The girls are I are going to the Santa Monica pier tonight and they wanted to know if you could join us. I know it's last minute. Sorry. So call us if you get the message. If not tonight, maybe we could do something tomorrow night. Um, if you're free."

"Hi, Miss Vanessa!" the girls both yell into the phone. "Call us!"

I hang up the phone feeling worried.

And afraid that Vanessa won't be calling me. Ever again.

EASTBROOKE ACADEMY – CONNECTICUT
RILEY

WE DROP OFF our bags at the hotel and go straight to Eastbrooke.

"I'm surprised we even got a room," Dallas says as we pass through the gates.

"Tyler can work miracles and somehow managed to find us a suite. But for all I know, we may be sleeping together in one bed," I tease.

"Like old times," Dallas says, grinning.

Of course, Tyler would never allow that. I know it's a large multi-bedroom suite, one for each of us, with a large living space to hang out in.

Keatyn glances at her watch. "It's getting late. We're going to have to hurry, so we don't miss the start of the game!"

Once we get out of the car, Dallas says, "Keatyn and I

will get us checked in. Do you want to come or would you like to be alone?"

"Why don't you two go," I say. "I think I'd like to be alone. Just for a few minutes."

"Are you okay?" Keatyn asks.

"Yeah, go. I'll be fine."

I must be a glutton for punishment because I'm not drawn to all the happy places, I'm drawn toward the spot.

The spot where it happened.

We had graduated, thrown our caps into the air, and posed for a million photos.

I pick her up, twirl her around, and kiss her.

When I set her down, she's crying.

All the girls have been super emotional today about leaving Eastbrooke and their friends, so I say, "Don't cry, Kitty. Just think, next week we'll be on the beach in California getting married."

She grabs my face tightly in her hands and kisses me. "I love you, Riley. I always will. No matter what happens. Please, don't ever forget that."

"I love you too, the soon-to-be Mrs. Johnson."

She holds her stomach like she might get sick.

"Are you okay?"

She just stares at me, tears flooding her eyes and mascara dripping down her face.

"I'm not going to California, Riley. I'm going to Princeton."

"What?!" I smile and flip her hair. "You're messing with me, aren't you?"

"No, Riley, I'm not. I have to go. My parents are waiting for me." She grabs my face and studies it like she's never going to

see it again. "Goodbye, Riley."

She turns her back on me and walks away.

My feet stay planted in this spot for what feels like an eternity, waiting for her to turn around.

For her to run back to me and jump into my arms and tell me she's just messing with me.

That it was some kind of silly graduation prank.

But she doesn't. She walks directly to her parents' car, gets in the backseat, and shuts the door as they pull away.

Not once does she look back.

I stand in stunned silence, trying to process the reality of it.

The finality of it.

Keatyn bounds toward me and wraps her arm around my neck. "Where's Ariela? You two ready to party? Can you believe next week you'll be getting married? My little Riley fell in lurve at Eastbrooke and now he's getting married."

"Ariela left," I say, barely able to string the words together. Barely able to comprehend the thought.

"Where'd she go?"

"Princeton."

"Wait, what?"

"She's not going to California."

Keatyn's demeanor changes and she grabs my hand. "What happened?"

"I don't know. She said she's going to Princeton. Told me goodbye. Then she got in her car and left."

"Oh, Riley," Keatyn says, tears filling her eyes. "I'm sorry."

I nod, still in shock, not letting go of her hand as she drags me across campus to her car.

"Call her, please," I beg.

She does.

"Voicemail." Then she grabs my phone and tries. "She's not

answering."

"Her dad told me I'd never amount to anything. I laughed and said watch me. *I think he got the last laugh."*

I look around. Visions of her are everywhere.

She was my world.

Sometimes I wish I could be young again. Do it all over. Fall in love for the first time. Feel the exhilaration. Count down the minutes of class just so I could kiss her again. Touch her face. See her smile. Feel the pride I felt whenever I walked through the halls with my arm wrapped around her.

I look down toward Hawthorne House where my dorm room was. I remember sneaking out and meeting her at the lacrosse field, some nights just holding hands and staring at the stars.

That's what I miss most about her.

Just holding her hand, not having to say a word, but knowing she felt the same way I did.

Or at least I thought she did.

"THIS IS THE spot, isn't it?" Keatyn asks, bringing me back to the present.

"Yeah."

"Are you okay, Riley? Was this a bad idea?"

I wrap my arm around her in a hug, partly because I appreciate what she's trying to do and partly because I just need a hug.

"Part of me feels like that eighteen year old. The feelings are still raw. But now I have ten years of maturity. We were young. There were signs. She'd kiss me and start crying. She said she was stressed about finals. I should have known something was wrong."

"I was thinking the same thing too," she says. "I remember that she was barely eating, but just blamed it on stress. Katie and I were a little worried she might be pregnant or anorexic, but we never would have guessed what she had planned." She shakes a red and gold pompom in front of my face. "You ready to go cheer Eastbrooke to victory?"

I falter.

Keatyn smacks her forehead. "I'm sorry. Shit. I remember what she did for you before the Homecoming game. With the pompoms."

"Ariela and I talked about that—the uh, the night we—"

"The TLF night?" Dallas asks, joining us.

"TLF?"

"True love's fuck," Dallas says.

"Okay, I've had enough memory lane. Let's go have fun," I say, but it's a front. Everywhere I turn—everywhere I look—I see memories of her. Memories of us.

And I'm torn between remembering them fondly and wishing I could get a quick case of amnesia to banish them away forever.

ONCE WE'RE SEATED, a familiar face plops down on the bleacher next to me. "Gracie, what are you doing here?"

"I'm thinking of enrolling," she says.

Keatyn is surprised to see her. "Does Mom know you're here?"

"Of course she does." She turns to me. "Oh, look, Baylor is wearing your old number, Riley. He's only a sophomore, but he's the starting quarterback. We've been texting since I visited a few weeks ago."

"Is that why you're really here, Gracie? For a boy?" Dallas asks her.

"Do you or do you not always say Eastbrooke was where you had some of the best times of your lives?"

"We do," Keatyn admits.

"That's why I'm considering it. End of story."

"And it has nothing to do with whatever is going on with you and Brady?" Keatyn asks.

"Of course not. Brady and I *were* friends. Now, *we're not*. It's as simple as that."

"But—" Keatyn starts to say.

"Speaking of butts," Gracie interrupts. "Check out number twelve's."

I laugh. For the first time since we arrived, I laugh. Gracie cracks me up. I've never met anyone who can so smoothly manipulate a conversation.

Actually, I take that back. I have. Gracie is a mini Keats.

"You sure you want to go to high school, Gracie?" I ask her. "A script came across my desk yesterday that made me immediately think of you."

"I already told you, Riley. No cheesy romances for me."

"This one isn't cheesy. It could be the next *Titanic*. A critically acclaimed box office hit. It's a big sweeping love story—sort of a Romeo and Juliet type of thing. Period piece. Young princess whose father wants her to marry the prince of their neighboring country to bring them peace—but she is in love with a young soldier."

"Sounds cool," she says, noncommittally as she stands up to cheer. "I think I want to be a cheerleader. Go Cougars!"

"What? No!" Keatyn screeches. "You have to be on the dance team!"

"I thought you didn't think I should go to Eastbrooke?"

"If you decide to come here, you have to be on the dance team, Gracie. And you need to know they have a lot of rules here. I know you complain you don't get to do as much as your sisters, but Mom and Tommy are pretty liberal."

Dallas and I laugh out loud. "You're one to talk, Keats. You always believed rules were for other people."

And in that moment, I stop seeing just me and Ariela and start remembering everything else.

The friendships.

The laughter.

The pickup lines Dallas used.

Screwing around in the football locker room.

Dallas trying to guess the color of girls panties.

How our goal in life was to get laid.

The parties at The Cave.

The nights we spent chilling at our secret party place, Stockton's.

The ceremony when the seven of us—me, Ariela, Maggie, Logan, Keatyn, Aiden, and Dallas—became Eastbrooke prefects.

When I threw a perfect deep pass to Aiden in the last few seconds of a rivalry game to seal our victory.

A little girl behind us taps Gracie on the shoulder and asks for her autograph. Gracie signs her program, takes a picture with her, and returns her attention to the game.

"I don't know much about football, but I can appreciate their uniforms," she says as the quarterback throws the ball down the field to a wide-open teammate for the score.

Dallas nudges me and nods toward a cheerleader, who's cheering more than the others. She's also wearing the quarterback's number on her cheek.

"Gracie, why is that guy texting you if he has a girl-friend?" Dallas asks.

"He doesn't have a girlfriend," she says.

I point to the cheerleader. "I think maybe he does."

Gracie narrows her eyes as Keatyn says, "Speaking of texting, I just texted Mom and she had no idea you were here."

Gracie shrugs. "I told her I was going to a football game."

"Yes, you just failed to mention that the football game was in *Connecticut*. How did you get here anyway?"

"Hitchhiked."

Keatyn gives her the eye.

"Fine. I hitched a ride on The Summer Boys jet. I'm considering dating Jared. Or Dylan, depending."

"Gracie, those boys are like twenty years old!"

"No, they're not. Jared is nineteen, and Dylan just turned seventeen."

"You're fourteen!"

"I'll be fifteen in a month. So, basically, I already am. And that's another reason why you should want me to come here, so I'll date boys my own age. Although, the band is fun to party with and I never get carded when I'm with—" She slaps her hand over her mouth.

I whisper to Keatyn, "You know if you have a girl she's going to be just like Gracie. Just like you."

"No, she won't. She'll be smart and responsible like Aiden."

I raise my eyebrow at her. Aiden was not adverse to partying and hooking up before he fell for Keatyn.

She shakes her head. "One step at a time. Mom and

Tommy have had it so easy with the triplets. They never get in trouble."

"That's not true," Gracie says. "The cleaning lady found cocaine in Ivery's room."

"What?!"

"Mom didn't want to tell you once she found out you're pregnant."

"Shhh," Keatyn says.

"It's not like everyone can't tell anyway. All they have to do is look at your stomach."

Keatyn touches her stomach, which still looks flat to me.

"You know we don't want people to know yet, Gracie."

Gracie rolls her eyes and gives Keatyn a little hug. "You know I'm just teasing."

"Where were you planning on staying tonight?"

"It's Homecoming. Party all night, right? And I have a date for the dance."

"You do?!" Keatyn asks.

"Yep," she smiles and nods at the field.

"The quarterback? He asked you?" I say.

"Do you think I would have come all this way to surprise him if he hadn't?"

Dallas and I share a worried glance.

This feels like the beginning of a major conflict scene in one of our teen movies.

"You're surprising him?" Dallas asks, on the same train of thought as I am.

She bounces in her seat. "I told him I didn't think I could make it but that I'd try. He'll be so surprised!"

"I bet he will be," Dallas says, nudging me.

"Riley, I think I need a hotdog," Keatyn says, suddenly grabbing my arm. "Come get one with me."

I BUY US both hot dogs and hand one to her. "I have a feeling the quarterback is going to have two dates."

"That's what I was thinking," she says. "Shit. Gracie is always such a good girl. Spunky and opinionated, but I didn't think she'd ever flat out disobey Mom and Tommy."

"Sounds like she didn't exactly disobey tonight." I grin.

"And hanging out with a band!"

"Twisted Dreams," I cough, reminding her that she hung out with a band when she was a teen too.

Her expression and eye roll is an exact match for the one the Gracie made a few minutes ago. "He was my best friend since we were kids. Not someone I met backstage at the teen awards."

"Sure you aren't mad at her because she broke up with Brooklyn's nephew?"

Tears threaten her face immediately. "Maybe. I miss Brooklyn so much. I still can't believe he's dead."

"Me either," I say, Brooklyn was a three-time pro surf champion who died in a surfing accident just a few years ago, was Keatyn's first love, and one of my best friends.

"I thought she and Brady would be together forever."

"She's fourteen, Keatyn. Do you really think she needs to decide on her forever love now?"

"Yeah, you're right. At her age, I was pretty boy crazy. She's so mature about her career, sometimes I forget how young she is."

"Do you know what they got in a fight about?"

"No, she won't tell anyone. Or at least she won't tell me."

"Maybe because she thinks you won't be on her side."

Keatyn's arm immediately goes up to her chest, offended. "I'll *always* be on her side!"

"Maybe you should tell her that."

She sighs big. "Yeah, I suppose you're probably right."

"What the fuck, Keatyn?" a familiar voice says. "You give my brother a cushy job but you can't pick up the phone and call your favorite Johnson brother? I want to live on the beach in California and drive a Ferrari too."

"Brax!" Keatyn yells, excited to see my youngest brother, who adores her. "I didn't think you were coming!"

"Change of plans," he says, slapping me on the back. "Good to see you, bro. You finally get up the balls to come back here?"

"Braxton!" Keatyn scolds.

"What? You know I'm right. You say so every year."

Keatyn's face turns pink. "I don't say that. Not exactly." I raise an eyebrow at her. "Fine. Every year I do mention that I wish you would get over it and come with us. It's not the same without you, Riley. You're such a big part of why Eastbrooke is so special to me."

I can't help but smile at her. "I'm glad I'm here this year."

"You are? Oh, Riley, that makes me so happy."

"Okay, jeez, enough with the love fest," Braxton says. "Let's get back to me and my cushy job."

"How are you doing?" Keatyn asks him. He and his long-time girlfriend just recently called it quits.

"I'm enjoying the spoils of single life again. Wine, women, and song. Okay, maybe more like beer, women, and meaningless sex."

"Thataboy," I tell him. "Just like a Johnson."

"Braxton, if you want a job, you'll have to convince your brother. He's in charge."

Braxton puts his arm around her. "Come on, Kiki. You

know you love me. And we all know who wears the pants at Captive. Riley didn't even know you hired Dawson."

"That was an unusual situation," Keatyn says with a frown.

"Which I fully supported," I say, backing her up, knowing it was hard for her to keep it from me.

"Speaking of love," Keatyn says. "Did you get your invitation to the party next weekend, Brax?"

"I did. I'm still checking to see if I can get out of work on Friday. Is it a big deal? You're always having fundraisers."

"Not fundraisers where Aiden and I get married."

"No, shit? It's about fucking time."

"I know. So come, please, if you can."

"I will. Who's winning?"

"We are," I say as we head back to the stands.

THE GAME ENDS with the Cougars winning by three touchdowns.

"You're going to stay with us at the hotel," Keatyn tells Gracie. "Not stay out all night."

"Whatever. I'm going to surprise Baylor now! He's going to be so happy!" she says rushing off.

"This ought to be good," Dallas whispers to me.

"What should be?" Braxton asks.

"The quarterback asked Gracie to Homecoming. She told him she didn't think she could make it and is surprising him."

"What's wrong with that?"

"One of the cheerleaders has his number on her face."

"Ooh, cat fight. Love those," Braxton says. "But Gracie's my girl. If he fucks her over, he's going to have to answer to me."

"Us too," Dallas agrees.

We watch as she runs down onto the field, taps him on the shoulder, and says *Surprise!*

"He definitely looks surprised."

"Oh, he's giving her a hug," Keatyn says.

"That's a good sign, isn't it?" I ask.

"Depends," Braxton says. "Check out the cheerleader at three o'clock. She's heading his way and she's got the march."

"What's the march?" Keatyn asks him.

"You know. The mad, pissed off girl march."

I laugh. "You're right. She does."

We continue to watch as the cheerleader grabs the quarterback's arm.

"She just said *What the fuck, Chad?*" Braxton says. "I can read lips."

"She definitely said what the fuck, but his name is Baylor. Baylor Hawthorne," Dallas says.

"As in *Hawthorne House* Hawthorne?" I ask.

"Yeah. His grandfather is on the Eastbrooke trust committee with me. He's only a sophomore. Good kid. Great athlete."

"Oh, boy. The cheerleader slapped him across the face and marched away!" Braxton says. "She looks sad. I should go comfort her. Excuse me."

I grab the back of his shirt. "Don't you dare, Brax. She's not exactly legal."

"Looks legal enough."

"Where are you staying tonight, Braxton?" Keatyn asks him.

"It's Homecoming. I'm partying all night," he replies. "Aren't you?"

"Actually, I'm kinda tired," Keatyn says. "It's been a really long week."

"It's been a long week for all of us," Dallas agrees.

"Pussies. How bout you, bro? You ready to scope out some of the alum? If I can't go young, maybe I'll look for a cougar. I've never done one before."

I shake my head. It's official. I'm getting old.

I don't even want to attempt to keep up with my younger brother.

Or maybe Vegas just cured me from partying for a while.

Gracie appears to have a serious conversation with the quarterback then leads him in our direction.

"Baylor, this is my sister, Keatyn Douglas," she says. "And her friends from Eastbrooke, Riley Johnson and Dallas McMahon."

"Don't forget me," Braxton says, popping up behind her.

"Brax!" Gracie screams. "My favorite Johnson brother! I'm taking you up on your offer to hang out in the Hamptons this summer."

"That'd be cool," Baylor says. "My grandparents have a place there. We could hang out."

If Gracie is thrilled by his invitation, you'd never know it. She just gives him a quick smile.

"I saw the movies," Baylor says. "Pretty cool to meet you all. So, does Stockton's really exist? Because we've all been down in the basement of the chapel and there is a Mary Jane Stockton crypt, but the leaf doesn't open, so there's no place for a key. No one can figure out how to get in."

"We may have changed some details to protect the innocent," I say.

"Or maybe we completely made it up," Dallas goes.

Keatyn adds with a smile, "Or, maybe it's a little of both."

"Damn, we could use a place to party besides The Cave."

"You go to The Cave?" Keatyn asks him. "Usually that's only for upperclassmen."

Baylor shrugs in a way that reminds me of Aiden when he was at Eastbrooke. When you're a star athlete, good-looking, and rich, exceptions are made.

"We had plenty of fun there," Keatyn says. "And even though we thought we were the only ones who knew about it, we found out later it's really not a secret."

"Baylor is taking me there tonight," Gracie says. "I can't wait."

"Um, Baylor, I'm curious," Keatyn says. "Why did that girl just slap your face?"

He lets out a breath and shrugs. "That's Krissy. She asked me to Homecoming, but I told her I already had a date. Today at our lunch table, I was telling my friend I was bummed that Gracie couldn't come. I'm sure glad she did though," he says, smiling at Gracie and wrapping his arm around her waist.

"So she just assumed you'd go together or did you tell her that you would?" Keatyn asks, trying to clarify the situation.

"I told her if I didn't have a date we could go."

"Typical girl," Braxton says. "Always reading too much into it."

"Oh, really," Gracie says, putting her hands on her hips, looking like a force to be reckoned with.

Braxton rubs the top of her head. "Chill out, Gracie."

"Well, it was nice to meet you all," Baylor says. "You ready to go have some fun, Gracie?"

"Of course," she says, linking her arm in his.

"Where were you planning to stay, Gracie?" Keatyn asks again.

"Hadn't gotten that far," she replies. "Figured I'd just crash somewhere."

"Why don't *I* make sure she gets back to the hotel," Braxton offers. "You at the usual place?"

"Yeah, except we have a suite this time," I reply.

"Penthouse?" Braxton asks. "Change of plans, kids. Party at the Penthouse."

Both Baylor and Gracie look excited until Keatyn says, "No party at the penthouse. Just sleep."

"Do you have room for all of us?" Gracie asks.

"We have room for you, *Gracie*," I stress.

"Not your bro?" Braxton asks. "I'm crushed."

"You can have the couch. And if you're so inclined, you and Baylor can share."

"Uh, sorry, man," Braxton says to Baylor. "Alright, old people. See you in the a.m."

WE HANG OUT for a bit after the game to chat with old friends, many of whom are genuinely happy to see me.

Finally, Dallas says to me, "I promised Aiden I'd make sure Keatyn got enough rest. If you want to stay, I can take her now and you can come back whenever you're ready. You put her through a lot this week and she looks exhausted."

I study her. She's smiling and speaking animatedly, but there are dark circles under her eyes and she keeps covering her mouth, trying to stifle her yawns. I feel bad for all I put them both through this week. "Yeah, she does. I'll go get her."

I interrupt her conversation. "Dallas is being a party pooper and wants to head to the hotel. You okay with that?"

She gives me a wide, happy smile. "Yes. I am."

ONCE WE'RE IN the car, she says, "Don't you think it's a strange twist of fate that the boy who I was supposed to babysit at The Cave when he came for Prospective Student Weekend is now watching my baby sister? Are you sure we shouldn't stay? Looking back, I did a really bad job of watching Braxton."

"Did he make it back to Dawson's dorm room that night?" I ask her.

"Yes."

"Then you did fine."

"He was shit-faced and puked all over a girl!"

"She puked on him back. It was even."

"I don't want Gracie drinking. She's too young."

"Ah, don't worry about it, Keatyn," Dallas says with a grin. "They'll probably sneak back to his dorm room to make out."

"Oh, that's even worse. Let's have the driver turn around. Dallas, are you really that tired?"

"No, but you are," he says.

"You guys tricked me?"

"Aiden said we'd probably have to," Dallas says. "And he was right."

"Just text Braxton," I suggest. "You know, if Braxton can handle Gracie, I might just give him a job. I could use someone to babysit some of our movie sets."

"Speaking of movie sets, did you know that Knox sees Jennifer as a very short term thing?"

"Really? That surprises me."

"Doesn't surprise me," Dallas says. "Knox liked that she crushed on him. He has a huge ego."

"It might even be bigger than yours," Keatyn says, teasing me.

"No way he's bigger than me," I tease back.

Keatyn's phone buzzes and she looks down at it.

"Shit. Your brother texted me back. He said *All's good*. Isn't that Johnson code for it's out of control but no one got arrested? Yet."

"Pretty much," Dallas laughs.

KEATYN FALLS ASLEEP on the couch while Dallas and I are flipping through TV channels.

"What do you think I should do about Ariela?" I ask him for the first time.

"What do you want to do?"

"I really don't know."

"How was being back?"

"Hard. At first, anyway."

"How so?" Dallas is like a shrink. He asks a whole lot of questions and never offers an opinion unless you force him to. And, to be honest, I probably don't want his opinion right now.

I slump down in my chair.

"We have a big balcony," he says, pulling a joint out of his pocket.

I set my scotch down. "Heck, yeah, we do. Shh. Be quiet. We don't want Keatyn to wake up."

"I'm still awake," she says. "Just resting my eyes. It seems wrong that I'm not going out to smoke with you. Especially here."

"We don't have to," I say, not wanting her to feel left out.

"Close the door, call me, and put me on speaker. That way I'll feel like I'm out there."

Dallas and I go out on the deck, light up, and do as we're told.

"Remember the morning when you called me and asked me how to get un-high fast?" Dallas says to Keatyn into the phone.

"Ohmigawd," Keatyn replies. "That was the morning I accidentally ate one of Jake's brownies before school. What about senior year when you tried to turn a hollowed out log into a party bong?"

"Aw, that's just a Southern boy trick."

"Nothing I'd ever seen, that's for sure." I add, laughing. "Remember after Prom, Ariela—"

"Uh, yeah," Dallas says. "Back to Ariela. How did being back here feel?"

"I could see her face everywhere. It made me really sad until about the middle of the game."

"What happened at the game?"

"You two. Coming back became more about all the fun times. Remember our Sunday morning powwows? Always just the three of us."

"We need to do that more often, I think," Dallas says. "Captive was always about the three of us. It's gotten so big. I know it makes the stockholders happy, made us all wealthy, but . . ."

"What are you thinking?"

"What if we sold off pieces of the business? We had a really lucrative offer come in today from a major player."

"We've had offers before. We always turn them down,"

I say.

"Not like this one. And they want to absorb us completely. I did a little digging and found out what they really need is our revenue stream. What if we carved out a few projects and employees we want to keep, negotiate to keep the name, and go back to being a boutique studio?"

I take another hit and pass him back the joint. "We always seem to make our life decisions this way, don't we? Smoking and talking."

"How would *you* feel about it, Riley?" Keatyn asks gently.

And I know what's she's thinking. She just offered me the chairman job. Something I've worked hard for. "Could I still be Chairman of Captive?" I ask playfully.

"Of course," Dallas says. "We'd still have our same roles, just have a whole lot less on our plates. More time to golf. And a much fatter bank."

"I'd want to take *Daddy's Angel* and my undeveloped scripts with me," Keatyn says. "And I have an idea."

She tells us about Knox's script and how they want to buy a neighboring farm to build a set.

"If we haven't signed anything with him yet, we won't need to address it in the deal. I think that sounds like a really cool project," Dallas says. "But back to Ariela. We keep getting off track."

"When we go back home, I'm going to call her," I say, surprising myself.

"I think that's a good idea," Dallas says. "What are you going to talk to her about?"

"Well, why her husband was kissing her, for starters. Then about being here. And probably about what's next. How do we move forward? How do we move past it?"

"Shit!" Keatyn says. "I just got a text from your brother. I knew we shouldn't have left!"

"What happened?" Dallas asks calmly as he takes another hit.

"I don't know. I think maybe he's drunk."

"He probably is!" I laugh. "What did he say?"

"He just said *cat fight* and *MEOW*. You don't think Gracie got in a fight, do you? Should we go back?"

A few minutes later, there's a knock on our hotel room door.

Dallas quickly puts out the joint, while I wave my hands to dissipate the smoke.

"It's Braxton," he says, looking through the window. We go inside to see what's going on.

Braxton is coming through the door with Gracie and Baylor in tow. Gracie's holding a towel to her cheek.

"What happened!?" Keatyn shrills.

Braxton sniffs the air. "I see you've all been having fun while I was babysitting the kids."

"You weren't babysitting me," Gracie says, then she looks directly at Keatyn. "*Was he?*"

"Do you really think if I thought you needed babysitting I'd leave you with Braxton?"

"Hey!" he says.

Keatyn just grins at him.

"I'm really sorry, baby," Baylor says to Gracie, causing me to immediately hate him. Because *baby?*

Dallas must not like it either because he grabs the little piss ant Hawthorne boy by the neck.

"I think we should have a chat," he says, pulling him out on the deck and telling him to sit.

I follow.

Towering above him, Dallas says, "What the fuck is your deal, son?"

His voice is so authoritative I almost tell him what my deal is.

"I don't have a deal, sir," Baylor replies. "I'm sorry Krissy hit Gracie. She was mad at me."

"Are you fucking her?" Dallas asks him.

"Gracie? What?! No!"

"He means the cheerleader," I say.

"Oh. Uh, Kinda."

"Kinda?" Dallas asks, still using his intimidating voice and reminding me of the teachers I had at military school. "Either you are or you aren't. Or else you just ain't very good at it. Which is it, boy?"

"Yes, I've slept with her. She's a junior. Pretty. I mean . . ."

"Does Gracie know this?"

He lowers his head and shakes it.

"Why did you ask Gracie to Homecoming? Or was that just bullshit talk that you got caught on?"

He looks up, surprise on his face. "No, sir. I was serious when I asked her. She's amazing. And she gets me. Gets the pressure of having a last name everyone knows."

"I see," Dallas says. "Very well, then. Why don't you get back inside."

The second he's gone through the door, Dallas lies across the couch and giggles. "It's hard being a hard ass when you're high."

"You did good. Reminded me of military school."

"Do you think he's telling the truth or do you think he knew we were high and could lie to us?"

I pull the door open and holler for my brother. "Braxton, get out here."

Keatyn follows him onto the deck, waving her hand in front of her face to make sure the smoke is gone.

"Tell us what really happened," Dallas says, sitting back up on the couch.

"Well, Gracie and Baylor—cool kid, by the way—were sitting by the fire. Chilling. Snuggling. Then Gracie went to get a beer—"

"Did you stop her?" Keatyn asks. "She's fourteen!"

Braxton slings his arm around her. "Keatyn, baby, if she's going to Eastbrooke, she's gonna have a beer occasionally. You did."

"I know, but . . ."

"Anyway," Braxton continues. "That's when the girl walked up and said something bitchy to her and Gracie said something back and the girl punched her."

"What did she say?"

"That she'd been sleeping with Baylor."

"Oh," Keatyn says, holding her stomach. "I should be easier on her. I know how that hurts."

"Gracie's a good kid, Keatyn. And she didn't take her shit. She told her that she didn't have to sleep with him to get a date. That's when she got pissed and hit her. But, it was Braxton to the rescue! I grabbed Gracie and pulled her away. And now we are here."

"What did Baylor do?"

"He was mortified. Which should say something about his character, because I would have been fucking thrilled if two chicks were fighting over me."

"I just don't want her to lose herself in a boy," Keatyn says.

Something inside me clicks.

"Did I do that?" I ask them. "With Ariela?"

"Um, well, uh . . ." Keatyn stammers. "You two *were* attached at the hip."

"More like the dick," Dallas chuckles. "I used to say she had your dick on a leash."

Keatyn swats Dallas. "Be nice."

Dallas giggles. "Hey, just being honest."

She turns to me. "But if we're being honest, we did call you Rileyella as if you were one person. Other than our Sunday morning powwows, you were rarely apart."

"Isn't that what monogamy is all about?" I ask.

"Consumed and monogamy aren't the same thing. But everyone thought you were the perfect couple. Everyone was so excited when you won Prom King and Queen."

"You can't really talk," I say to Keatyn. "You and Aiden are the perfect couple."

"No, we're not. Aiden and I are happy but our relationship has always been plagued with imperfection. I think that's part of what makes it special. We have so many personal interests that could tear us apart. The worst was after college when he and Logan played pro soccer. He was traveling more than I was."

"I clearly remember the two of you sneaking off at parties in high school and beyond."

"Sure, we'd sneak off, but we'd have some quick fun then come back. You and Ariela never came back."

"Ever," Dallas emphasizes.

"You never know what path life is going to lead you down," Braxton says, philosophically. "But that's the fun part. Enjoying the ride, right?"

"Maybe you and Ariela needed this time apart, Riley," Keatyn adds. "Maybe you needed to grow stronger as individuals. Maybe if she would have come to California, you wouldn't be as successful as you are now."

"You might be right about that," I say thoughtfully. "Although, I think I was more wrapped up in my dream for us than I was in our reality. You know how fans want Aiden's point of view? His side of the story? That's what I wish I had. I wish I could read her journal from back then, so I could understand what I missed. Understand what she was going through. Was I so wrapped up in my dream that I ignored hers? I've rehashed it over and over in my head, wondered what I should have done differently."

"Riley, the problem with you and Ariela is your story is left untold. You need to know the ending."

"Do you agree with Keatyn's assessment?' I ask Dallas.

"I think the better question is can you handle the ending? Whatever it is."

"I'm not sure, but I do know one thing."

"What's that?"

"That I don't know what I'd do without the two of you in my life. Those nights at Stocktons. Our epic parties. The stupid shit we did. It's amazing to me how those nights formed the basis for our long friendship."

Keatyn leans over and hugs me while Dallas says, "I'll drink to that. In fact, I think we should."

He goes inside then comes back out with four glasses on a tray. "Scotch for the men, sparkling water for the lady."

"Wait," Braxton says, "Why is Keatyn drinking water?"

Keatyn just smiles at him as we clink our glasses together and say, "To lifelong friendships."

Saturday, October 11th
HOTEL SUITE – CONNECTICUT
GRACIE

I'M LYING IN bed, listening to Keatyn talk to Aiden, pretending I'm still asleep. When she hangs up, I roll over and snuggle into her shoulder. "I don't have a dress to wear for the dance."

"You didn't bring a dress?"

"I did, but it's a long gown. Baylor was talking about gowns and I thought that's what they wore, but that was just for Homecoming Court last night. The girls are wearing short dresses for the dance. Really, it's just like it was in the movie. Short dress for the dance, then club clothes for the after party."

"You should've asked me, Gracie, I would have told you."

"I decided at the last minute to come."

"Why?"

I let out a long sigh in lieu of an answer. Because the answer is so complicated.

"Let me guess," she says. "It has to do with Brady."

I roll my eyes at the sound of his name. "Sort of."

"Why don't you tell me what happened. Maybe I can help."

"No," I say, shaking my head. "It's embarrassing."

"Gracie, you know you can tell me anything. I won't freak out like Mom will."

"That's for sure. Mom caught Brady and I making out and about had a fit. You'd think it'd be Dad, but Mom's gotten all uptight lately."

"Sounds like Ivery is having some trouble, huh?"

"Yeah, she's being stupid. Some of the girls she models with told her if she wanted to make it big, she needs to be skinnier. Told her cocaine and coffee was the way to do it. That's why she had the cocaine. She's not doing it. She thinks it's stupid. But instead of talking to her, Mom freaked out and assumed she is."

"A lot of times people lie about doing drugs, Gracie. Cocaine is very dangerous and very addictive. I can see why Mom would freak. And if she wasn't going to use it ever, why didn't she throw it away?"

"She says she forgot. Hmm, okay, I see what you're saying, because now you're making me wonder. But I believe her, just for the record. Mom threw it away, sat us all down, and threatened to bring in a drug dog. Surely, she knows how easy drugs are to get."

Keatyn closes her eyes tightly.

"I'm never doing them either. We were taught about healthy lifestyles. I'm vegan, most of the time. You think I want to screw up my body with drugs when I won't even eat a freaking hamburger?"

Keatyn laughs. "Probably not. So back to Brady, did he cheat on you?"

"He couldn't cheat on me because technically we weren't going out."

"You were together all the time."

"People call that *being friends*."

"So you are friends who kiss?"

"*Kissed,*" I state emphatically. "I will never, ever kiss him again." I sit up and cross my legs into a pretzel. "If I tell you, do you swear that you won't tell anyone? Especially not the triplets. They give me enough shit about him as it is."

"What do they give you shit about?"

"Maybe not shit, just unwanted advice. Avery feels I'm too young to be tied down to one boy. Ivery told me that if I didn't sleep with him, he'd sleep with someone else. And Emery said I should make it exclusive."

"I'm confused about that, because I thought you were exclusive."

"For the last two years, we've been best friends. That's all. But in the last few months, we started holding hands and kissing and stuff. Then he told me he loved me and that he wanted us to do more. That we should be each other's firsts. And I love him, I mean *loved* him, but I just . . ." I can't stop the tears even though I vowed not to cry one more stupid tear over him.

Keatyn takes my hand and pats it. "Did you do it with him?"

"No, I didn't. I told him I wasn't ready."

"Is that what the fight was about?"

"No, he told me he'd wait until I was ready." Tears keep rolling down my face, which pisses me off. I quickly brush them away. "But he didn't."

Keatyn's eyes get big. "Did he force you?"

"What?! Oh, gosh no. He wouldn't." I cover my face

with my hands. "He did it with someone else. Guess who? *Kylie*."

"But she's your best friend!"

"*Was* my best friend."

"Oh, Gracie," she says, wrapping me in a hug. "I'm so sorry. When did all this happen? You were together at the movie premiere."

"After the premiere, I visited Eastbrooke. Brady was being a baby about it. Said he didn't understand why I couldn't just go to school with him and Kylie and the rest of our friends. Then when I got home, he complained that I barely texted him while I was here. I explained that I was busy and trying to see what life here would be like. Then he started kissing me, telling me he loved me, that he didn't want me to leave him, and made me feel guilty for even considering it. Then he told me it was time. That he didn't want to wait anymore. That if I really loved him, I would do it with him. That he needed to know I loved him." I stop and take another deep breath. "I was going to, but he wasn't acting like himself. He was being forceful and it just felt . . . wrong. When I yelled at him and told him to stop, he about started crying. That's when he told me that he slept with Kylie while I was gone. I told him never to speak to me again."

"Have you?"

"Nope."

"And?"

"He keeps texting me, begging me to reply. To come surf with him. Says he misses me. That I'm his best friend. That he's so sorry. That she doesn't mean anything to him. But he's a liar. He's still hanging out with her. She posted pictures of them together on her Instagram. So, needless to say, even though I don't give a shit what he does, I've been posting a few photos of my own." I grab my phone and show her a few of my favorites. "Here's me with the Summer Boys, backstage at one of their concerts. I like this one especially. Jared looks like he's totally into me."

Keatyn scrolls through my photos then tilts her head. "There's not one photo of you and Baylor."

"There are some on his phone. He made me take a selfie with him before I left." I blush. "He kissed me on the cheek."

"Why on the cheek?"

"Because I told him I had a boyfriend at home."

"When you met Baylor here, were you interested in him?"

"I see where you're going with this and you're right. The fact that I had fun with Baylor is also part of why I didn't sleep with Brady. There's just something about Baylor. Like when we met. It was weird."

"Weird how?"

"When I first got here, they set me up with Tiffany, a senior prefect. She was really cool and didn't let my being famous get in the way of things. Or maybe they told her not to. I'm not sure, but I felt as close to a normal kid as I ever have. Anyway, I sat with her at lunch." I smirk at her. "And yes, she sits at your table. Imagine how honored I was."

"Stop teasing me," she says, laughing.

"Anyway, this boy sits down across from me. Not at the same table, but at the one next to us and since no one is sitting across the table from either one of us, our eyes meet. God, that sounds corny. *Our eyes met from across the room.* But they did. And I mean, I couldn't help but notice how cute he was. Dark brown hair, bright blue eyes, and when he smiled at me, it wasn't like when most people smile at me. Like they recognize me, their eyes get big, and then they smile. He just smiled at *me*. He wasn't smiling at Gracelyn Stevens, the actress. He was smiling at Gracie, the girl. I sound ridiculous, don't I?"

"No, Gracie, you don't. You know what you felt and you should trust your judgement. Just like you knew it wasn't right for you to sleep with Brady. So, how did you start talking to him?"

"After lunch, I had to shadow a sophomore guy named Trent, so I could see what my classes would be like. He sits behind Baylor in math. Trent sat at his desk and wasn't sure where to have me sit because all the desks were full, so I was awkwardly standing there. Baylor stood and offered me his seat. Sounds stupid but it was sort of chivalrous. I was grateful to sit, but was also sad because it meant I wouldn't get to sit by him. But then I heard this horrible screeching noise and when I turned around, Baylor was dragging a chair toward me. We shared his desk and instead of taking notes, he was drawing funny little pictures that made me laugh. When class was almost over, he made this little cartoon of a floppy-eared dog holding up a sign asking for my number. We texted most of the day, and he invited me to hang out with him and his friends that night. When we walked toward the gym, he took my hand in his. I remember the first time Brady held my hand. It was awkward. Like he wasn't sure if he should. Baylor took my hand in his without question. It was sort of possessive. Which was kinda hot. But at the same time it felt . . . different. Like special different."

I look up at Keatyn, who is biting her lip, trying not to smile.

"Fine," I say. "To quote *The Keatyn Chronicles* movie,

My hand felt like it belonged in his forever."

"Oh, Gracie!"

I roll my eyes at her and grin. "Don't get all excited. I used to think I would marry Brady. Clearly, I don't know what the hell I want. Except for a dress."

"We need to go shopping. Let's see. If we skipped the tea, left for New York now," she says, looking up at the sky doing the math in her head. "Hmm. There's no way we could get there, find a dress, get back, and get you ready. I have a better idea." She picks her phone up off the bed. "I'm calling Kym."

"Oh, gosh, don't do that!" I tell her. Kym is one of my mom's best friends, as well as her and Keatyn's long-time stylist.

"Why not?"

"Because she'll tell Mom everything."

"What's there to tell? You're going to a dance."

"Yeah, I guess. Fine. I'm desperate."

"I'll put her on speaker."

We hear Kym answer with, "Keatyn, darling, how are you?"

"That depends on how you're doing finding me a wedding dress on such short notice."

"I'll have at least a dozen for you to try next week and a seamstress on site to make any alterations necessary. Are we still meeting at the vineyard on Friday afternoon?" Kym replies.

"Yes, providing all goes well on set this week. So, Kym, what are you doing today?" Keatyn asks casually.

"Oh boy," Kym says, immediately catching on. "Why does it sound like you need something last minute?"

"We do. Gracie is on the line with me. She got invited

to Homecoming at Eastbrooke and thought she was supposed to wear a gown instead of a cocktail dress. Do you have anything good in your office?"

"I always have something good in my office, Keatyn. Do you need hair and makeup too, Gracie?"

"Um, that would be nice," I say, looking down at my chipped nails.

"And a manicure," Keatyn says. "She needs something really cute."

"And preferably not *age appropriate*," I say.

"Your mother says all dresses must be age appropriate."

I give Keatyn my puppy dog eyes. I need her on my side.

Keatyn smiles at me then says, "Gracie knows that and agrees with her. But this isn't a public event. This is her first Homecoming. She needs something sophisticated. Something that's both sexy and a little edgy. The kind of dress that would knock a boys socks off." I bounce on the bed happily and silently clap my hands. "And while you're at it, bring her a really hot dress for the after party along with shoes she can dance in. We're at the usual hotel. Penthouse."

After she ends the call, I bounce toward her and give her an excited hug. "You are the best sister ever!"

"Gracie," she says seriously, holding my arms, "You can always tell me anything. I'm always here for you. Just because the triplets are a few years older than you, doesn't mean they have the life experience to give you good advice."

"Except for Avery," I laugh, because she always gives good advice.

"Except for Avery," she agrees as there's a knock on our door.

"You two decent in there?"

"Knox?" Keatyn's face crunches up in confusion. "What the hell?"

When the door opens, Riley and Knox both bound onto our bed. It seems sort of surreal sometimes to think my sister gets to sleep with Knox on screen and then go home to Aiden. My friend—I mean, my former friend—Kylie, used to say Keatyn was one lucky bitch.

"Gracie!" Knox says, rubbing his hand across my hair. "Heard you got in a fight last night."

"Meow!" Braxton says, joining us by flopping his body across the bed.

"What are you doing here, Knox?" Keatyn asks.

"He wishes he went to Eastbrooke," Dallas drawls from the doorway. "I told him not to come."

"But here I am anyway. Better than hitting Vegas again, don't you think?"

"I thought you had to work?"

"Got done early. Took the red eye. I heard you need a date for the dance," he says, batting his eyes at my sister.

"I already have two dates," she says, pointing toward Riley and Dallas.

"Fine," Knox says seriously, holding his hand to his heart. "I thought Riley might need some emotional support. I know what a trying time this is for him."

"Bullshit," everyone says at once, laughing.

"Fine. I thought maybe I could meet a woman here. A normal one."

"Ah, now the truth comes out," Braxton says. "I'll let you be my wingman. Brax will be on the prowl tonight too."

"Knox doesn't believe in being the wingman," Riley jokes.

"Gotta be in the limelight all the time," Dallas agrees,

while Keatyn nods her head and laughs.

"This is why I want to go to Eastbrooke," I say, although I didn't realize I said it out loud until Braxton says, "Speaking of Eastbrooke. Your boy is still crashed on the floor."

"He's not my boy," I say, even though I wish he were.

"I'm crushed," Baylor says from the doorway. God, how does he look so perfect in the morning? His hair is a little mushed to one side, but it just makes him look cuter. And those blue eyes and long, dark lashes.

Shit!

I realize that I have no flipping idea what I look like. "Uh, excuse me," I say, hopping out of bed and rushing to the bathroom.

When I shut the door, I realize how ridiculous I must have looked. Like a two-year old who was going to pee her pants.

But then I appraise myself in the mirror and am I glad I did. I mean, everyone has to pee, right?

I brush my teeth quickly and run a brush through my hair, wipe the mascara smudges off my cheek, and dab on some chap stick.

"Let's order breakfast!" Keatyn is saying as I come back out. She jumps up and grabs the hotel phone. "I'll just order a bunch of everything and we can share!"

I go toward the door. "Hey," I say, a little awkwardly to Baylor. I've never been allowed to spend the night with a boy before. Not that we spent the night together. I just mean I've never woken up and they've been there.

"Good morning," Baylor says, running his hand through his hair, trying to get it to lie flat. "Can we go out on the balcony for a minute?"

"Uh, sure," I say, following him. Damn. Is he mad at me because I said he's not my boy?

"It's chilly," he says, running back inside to grab a blanket off the chaise. He brings it out and wraps it around us.

"It is," I say as we sit down next to each other with our shoulders touching. Actually, it's more than our shoulders. It's all the way down our arms. "You're warm though."

"Gracie," he says. "I need to tell you something. Dallas asked me about it last night and it's all I've been thinking about. I know we're not going out or anything, but that girl, Krissy . . . I, um, have been sleeping with her. I think that's why she's mad about you being here. She's older and she's slept with a lot of guys, from what I understand. I only did it—god, I sound so lame—because I hadn't before. Most of my friends had done it last year. I had been waiting for someone special, but didn't want to be the only virgin. And Krissy was interested in me. And she's older. And I hadn't met anyone special—so, I just wanted you to know. Maybe you don't care. You probably don't. And now you probably hate me. If you do, I understand. I just wanted to be honest with you. I like you."

I frown, the thought of him with anyone disturbs me way more than I expect.

"I'm glad you told me," I say flatly.

"Um, what about your boyfriend?"

"I don't have a boyfriend anymore," I snap.

And, I swear, Baylor's blue eyes sparkle when I do. Not to mention the devastatingly handsome smile that spreading across his face.

"Bad breakup?"

I let out a sarcastic chuckle. "You could say that. He slept with my best friend while I was visiting Eastbrooke."

"Oh, wow. I'm sorry. Is that why you decided to come to Homecoming? Are you trying to get back at him?"

"No! Please don't think that. I came because—"

"Food's here!" Keatyn yells out the door, interrupting me.

"Because why?" Time feels like it stands still when he reaches up and touches my face, his blue eyes gazing intently into mine.

"Because I like you too."

HOTEL SUITE – CONNECTICUT
KEATYN

WE HAVE BREAKFAST then the boys go golfing while Gracie showers.

I get a call from my former Eastbrooke roommate, Katie. We were on the dance team together, she took Dallas' virginity, and was nicknamed Tigger because she was so bouncy. She's well-endowed and her boobs tend to bounce as much as she does. I haven't seen her since she came to California on spring break.

"I wish we were at Homecoming right now," she pouts.

"I'm actually here."

"What? You went without me?"

"Yeah, last minute. I'm with Riley."

"Oh, gosh. It's his first time back, isn't it? Maggie filled me in on what's been going on with him and Ariela."

"Did she tell you everything? Like about next weekend?"

"The party? I got the fancy invitation for the—wait! No, way! Are you and Aiden getting married?"

"Yes. I hope you can come."

"I'll be there for sure. Can I tell you a secret?"

"Yes."

"I hate my job."

"I thought you loved teaching?"

"I do," she says with a sigh. "Maybe it's that I hate myself. I gave in and slept with the hot young history teacher. Why can't I date guys my own age? Why do I keep falling for fresh out of college boys? Boys who need a mother more than they need a girlfriend. I mean, can they really not bother to pick up their underwear when they know I'm coming over?"

"I suppose it depends what time you're going over there and if their mom picks up after them."

"Oh! Shut up! That was one time!" She giggles. "Oh my god, I will never live that down, will I?"

"You never should've told us that his mom made you breakfast."

"Funny thing is, his mom and I are still friends! I had lunch with her the other day."

"Well, she is closer to your age than he is."

"She thinks I'm still in college. I always wear a ponytail when I see her. I'm horrible. So how's Riley doing?"

"He seems to be okay. Went golfing with the boys. He'll probably come back drunk enough not to care. And Knox showed up."

"That man is fine. Why can't I meet someone who looks like him?"

"If you come to the wedding, you can meet him."

"Oh, lord have mercy. I'll probably have a spontaneous orgasm. Or my ovaries will explode."

"When you meet him, you should ask him the question you always want me to find out the answer to."

"What I want to know is why in the world has no reporter ever asked him. It's the *one* question every woman in America wants to know, whether they'd admit to it or not."

"I dare you—no, I double dog with hot fudge on top dare you—to ask him."

"I can see it now. I have a few thousand glasses of wine, stumble toward him. He catches me in his arms and I ask him. Only he doesn't understand because I'm drunk and it sounds like *Knox, do you mumble mumble really and if we mumble mumble would you mumble mumble mine down lower?*"

"Katie! Oh my god! I thought you were going to ask if he bites a girl's lip when he kisses her in real life! Not if he does it when he goes down on her."

"You didn't know that's what I've always been talking about? Every time I see you two kiss on screen that's all I can think about. Him going down on me. Oh—shit, gotta go, my doorbell is ringing. The hot asshole history teacher is taking me to lunch."

"Well, that sounds sweet!"

"Okay, I lied. He's bringing lunch, but we won't eat it because he will attack me the second I open the door."

"And that sounds hot. Enjoy!"

"You too. Tell Foxy Knoxy that I'm coming for him."

I hang up the phone laughing as I let the hair and makeup team in, order some lunch from room service, and then get myself in the shower.

"WHAT DO YOU think?" Gracie asks, holding up her hands and showing off pretty, pale pink nails with black tips. "I got a fun French manicure. Subtle, but cute, right?"

"It's very pretty and will go with anything you wear."

I pay the hair and makeup team and let them out of the suite as Kym is coming down the hall with two bellmen in tow. It's already five o'clock, and I was starting to get worried she wasn't going to make it in time.

"Auntie Kym!" Gracie screeches, hopping up to give her a hug. "I haven't seen you in forever."

"I dressed you for the premiere just a few weeks ago!"

"Well, it feels like forever," Gracie smiles.

"You know how to work it, don't you? Trying to butter me up, so I'll let you wear something your mother wouldn't approve of?"

A Cheshire cat grin spreads across Gracie's face. "Maybe."

"I swear, you both smile just like your mother," she huffs, coming over to give me cheek kisses. "It just so happens there is nothing on these racks that she would approve of."

"Can I see?" Gracie asks, standing patiently by the door as the bellman leave, only to be replaced by Dallas, Knox, Riley, and Braxton, who are tipsy and sweaty.

"Well, if it isn't my favorite stylist," Knox drawls, giving Kym air kisses. "How's married life treating you?"

Kym finally tied the knot last summer after dating a real estate mogul for over five years.

"It's good. He's as busy as I am, working on a new business development in Dubai. We meet up for sex every week then go our separate ways. The perfect arrangement." She glances at Gracie then says, "You didn't hear that."

"My lips are sealed," Gracie says, pretending to zip her lip.

"I'm going to take a shower," Braxton says. "Keatyn, wanna join me?"

"Not this time, Brax, but thanks!" I say with a laugh.

"Your date, Baylor, is a good golfer. Like, really good," Dallas says to Gracie, as he makes Kym a drink.

"He beat Dallas for best ball every time," Riley chuckles as he flops onto the couch.

After Kym takes a sip, she rolls the clothes into the bedroom. "You all stay seated on the couch. Miss Gracie and I are going to put on a fashion show. You can help her decide what to wear."

"You know *she's* going to decide what she wants to wear," I say.

"She does have strong opinions, that's for sure," Kym agrees.

AFTER ABOUT TWENTY minutes, I'm getting worried that Kym didn't bring anything Gracie likes. But then the door opens and Gracie bounds out in a skintight embossed black halter dress with a plunging neckline.

"What do you think?" she asks, spinning around for us.

"Uh," both Dallas and Riley say. I think they are shocked to see that she has boobs. And her cleavage is fully on display in this dress.

"Love it," Knox says. "Is that for the after party?"

"It is," Kym says. A Cavalli mini dress with the Fendi Chunky Mixed-Media Hole Punch Sandal. We didn't do any jewelry because the dress says it all."

"What's the dress supposed to say?" Riley asks. "Because it looks really sexy. *Too* sexy."

Gracie starts jumping up and down and hugging Kym. "Yay! You made me look sexy. *Too sexy*! It's perfect! Come on, let's show them the dress for the dance," she says, dragging Kym back into the bedroom.

"What just happened?" Riley asks.

"You played into her hand," Knox says, setting his drink down. "She likes Baylor. She wants to look hot for him."

"She does," I agree.

"She's not supposed to look hot. She's like twelve!" Riley says.

"Fifteen!" Gracie yells from the bedroom.

"Fourteen!" I yell back, teasing her. "But Knox is right. She likes him."

Dallas lowers his voice. "Did you find out what happened with Brady?"

"He slept with her best friend after he told her they should lose their virginity to each other."

"Oh, I'm gonna kill that little bastard," Riley says. "What a fucking douche."

"Like you never told a girl anything she wanted to hear to get her into bed," Dallas says to Riley.

"I know *I'll* tell them anything," Brax says, walking out into the room wearing nothing but a towel wrapped around his waist.

"Speaking of grown up," I say to him, because last time I saw him in a swimsuit, he did not look like that.

He poses, almost losing the towel but grabbing it at the last second. "I was working out with Dawson before he ditched me for California. Put on a few pounds." He looks down at himself, satisfied. "And a few muscles. Wanna lick my abs?"

"Can we do body shots off them like in the movie?" Gracie asks, coming back out in another dress. I see now why she tried on the other one first. It makes this pale pastel one look demure in comparison, but it's really not.

"Pale peach Herve Leger bandage dress with rose gold

hardware. Adds a bit of an industrial element to the lingerie style," Kym says. "And walk, Gracie, so they can see the hem. I love how it flutters with the two-tone fringe. I've paired it with black wavy suede cutout booties by Sophia Webster."

Gracie stands in front of me. Her hair has grown out to almost a bob, but she's wearing long extensions tonight and looks even more grown up than usual.

I stand up and hug her. "You look beautiful, Gracie. It's the perfect dress."

"Your body is rocking, little Miss Gracie," Braxton says. "Baylor's jaw will drop to the floor when he sees you."

"Do you think so?" Gracie says, clasping her hands together and spinning in a circle. "I can't wait!"

"Keatyn, I'm going to touch up Gracie's makeup. Why don't you come try a few things on?" Kym suggests. "And boys, I shouldn't have to say it, but get ready."

"I'm almost ready!" Braxton yells. "That means I get to do a shot."

I point my finger at the rest of them, sprawled across the couches and worn out from golf and drinking all afternoon. "You better do as she says."

I'M DRESSED AND ready before the boys are, so I join Braxton back out in the living room. He looks very handsome and so different from how he used to.

"You look like a man," I tell him.

"I'm serious about a job. I know you think I just want to come out there and just fuck around, but I don't. I've already gotten two promotions where I'm at."

"You need to talk to your brother. I think he might have some ideas."

"Awesome."

"So, what happened with you and Embry? You were together for what—five, six years?"

"Since our senior year of high school. Made it through college together. I had even bought a ring."

"You did?!"

"Yeah. I mean, it's what was expected of us. We'd graduated college and everyone was asking when we were getting married. It seemed like the next step. But I'd had the ring for two months when she said she was going to Seattle without me. Every time I thought about proposing, something stopped me. So I think it was meant to be. Overall, she wants different things out of life than I do. She's so serious. Everyone always said that it was good we were opposites. I know opposites attract, but you still need to have the same basic core values, the same goals in life. She didn't know if she wanted to have kids. I don't want them right now, but I definitely want them. Family is important to me, even more so after what happened with Whitney. I spend a lot of time with my nieces. I'm totally their favorite uncle. Speaking of that, you didn't do a shot last night. You knocked up?"

I bite my lip, trying not to smile.

"Ha! Knew it!" he says. "Congratulations." He goes and pours two shots. "And to prove just how happy I am for you, I'll drink a couple shots in your honor."

"YOU LOOK SAD," Riley says as he sits down next to me.

"I'm watching my baby sister dance with a boy. She looks so pretty and grown up tonight. It seems like it wasn't that long ago that I used to rock her to sleep."

"My parents always say they blinked and we were all in

college. I think you're doing the right thing, taking time off after you have the baby. And I think we should take the offer to sell off Captive."

"I don't know if I could ever sell it, Riley. It's our baby."

"Yeah, and we blinked and now we're going to send it off to college. Dallas thinks we should take the offer too."

"I know he does and I don't want to downplay his role, but he hasn't invested in it the same way you and I have."

"We've invested in it with our lives. Don't you think it's time we get them back?"

"You know I want to slow down. It just sounds too perfect to be true."

He leans back and holds his arms out. "You know what they say about me. I'm the king of romance. It only makes sense that Captive Films gets a happily ever after ending too."

I smile at him.

"You look beautiful tonight, by the way. You really are glowing."

"This dress is a good color on me."

"It's more than that and you know it. You're happy. You're pregnant and marrying your true love in a week. It shows in your face. Except in the morning when Tyler brings you coffee."

"The other morning when I was getting my ass handed to me by the board, he brought me coffee. I lost it and yelled that I never wanted coffee again."

"What did he do?"

"Brought me back lemon tea and told me it helped his sister with her morning sickness. I hadn't told him. He just knew. I know you pay him well, but if we do this, I want to give him a really big bonus."

"Hopefully not so big that he won't want to keep working for the new and improved Captive," Riley says. "We need him."

"I know. And I want employment contracts for all of the employees. Something that states if they don't keep their jobs for at least two years, they get some sort of buyout."

"I think Dallas can negotiate that."

"Are you sure it will make you happy, Riley? You love your job. Love doing deals. We won't have that anymore."

"Deals are fun, but they aren't my passion. You know that."

"I didn't know if your passion has changed. You're a really good executive."

"If we do this smaller company, I want Dawson to take over as CEO. I'll help, but I want to produce again—"

He stops mid-sentence and stares into space.

"Earth to Riley."

"I think I know when it happened."

"What happened?"

"It was about three weeks before graduation. We were sitting here, just like this, at our year-end athletics banquet. Ariela went home that weekend and missed both it and our soccer game the next day."

"I remember the game. You kicked the winning goal, sending us to the playoffs."

"When I was at the banquet, she texted me. Just a sad face. When she got back, she cried about missing the banquet."

"You won a lot of awards."

"And she cried when she heard I kicked the winning goal and she missed it," I say.

"It wasn't the first or the last time you kicked a winning

goal."

"I know, that's why it was weird. I think it was more. I think that's when her parents must have told her whatever they did to convince her, or force her, to go to Princeton. It was her dad's dream. She studied like crazy to get good grades because of it. But what I don't get is why she would marry freaking Collin."

"Because he was there, probably. He liked her. Her parents liked him. It was the probably the path of least resistance."

"Sounds caveman of me, but all I can think about is that she slept with him."

"I think you two just dealt with it differently, Riley. You never let anyone in. She pretended to let someone in but didn't. It's hard to replace a once-in-a-lifetime love."

"Honest to God—no bullshit—do you think we could work now? After all this time? I'm such a different person than I was back then."

"I wish I could answer that. I think only you and Ariela can decide. When you slept with her, you said it was different. Did you sleep with anyone in Vegas?"

"More like many someone's," Dallas says, laughing and setting another drink in front of Riley.

"Actually, I didn't," he says.

"What do you mean?" Dallas asks. "Knox said you had two hookers in the bedroom, maybe three."

"We hooked up but I didn't have sex. I tried. I couldn't." He buries his face in his hand.

"What aren't you telling us?" I ask, touching his arm.

He points down at his pants. "*It* wasn't cooperating. I got pissed. Told the hooker it was her fault and I wasn't going to pay her. I think that's when she stole my wallet and ran out."

"Which then started the naked party parade."

"Yeah."

"You were probably just too drunk to maintain an erection, dude. It happens," Dallas says, slapping Riley on the back and then walking off to talk to someone else.

"But you know differently, don't you, Riley?" I ask.

"Yeah, I know it was because of her."

VANESSA'S ESTATE – HOLMBY HILLS
DAWSON

I'M NERVOUS AS I pull up to Vanessa's home in the Range Rover that showed up in my garage a few days ago, complete with a booster seat for Harlow. I've been so busy at work that I hadn't even realized that I couldn't fit the girls and their bags into the Ferrari. Thank goodness I mentioned they were coming to Tyler. He literally thinks of everything.

"This house looks like a castle," Harlow says, echoing my thoughts. "Is Vanessa a princess?"

"You'll have to ask her that," I say absent-mindedly. I knew Vanessa's ex-husband was wealthy, but I didn't expect this. My heart drops into my stomach, knowing I could never give her anything that compares to this. Even with what I'm earning now, I probably couldn't even qualify for a mortgage, not with a foreclosure on my credit history.

I remember the day so vividly. The girls crying and saying they didn't want to leave their house. *What if Mommy comes back and we aren't here?* Living with my parents was what we all needed though.

Although, I didn't know it at the time.

I was still in shock. I couldn't believe what my life had become. My wife had killed herself. I was broke, with two little girls to raise on my own. I didn't care about my job anymore and a had mess of financial disbelief. I couldn't face the reality of what Whitney had done.

Still can't, really.

But at least we're moving in the right direction.

"Dad, it says you have to press the button if you want the gate to open," Ava says, bringing me back to the present.

"Or you could say *Open Sesame!*" Harlow giggles from the backseat.

"Thanks, honey." I roll down the window and hit the call button. When Vanessa's butler answers and says, "May I ask who's calling?" the girls giggle again.

Harlow says, "We aren't calling, we're visiting."

"Dawson, Harlow, and Ava Johnson," I reply politely as the gate opens and we drive through it. "Remember, girls, you are to be on your best behavior."

"We will be," they sing.

"Grandma told us . . ." Harlow says.

"Harlow!" Ava warns.

"What were you going to say, Harlow?" I ask her.

"Grandma told us not to scare Miss Vanessa away. We won't, Daddy. We promise to be good."

I run my hand through my hair and take a deep breath. Clearly, it's time to have a chat with my family. I'm also praying the girls like the school we're visiting on Monday. I need them here with me.

Part of me wants to turn around and drive off. I don't know what I'm doing. Vanessa and I haven't been together since I told her about wanting to spend time alone with the girls. The tabloid article was right. I was chasing after her all night trying to figure how to make it up to her.

I was shocked when she called this morning, told me she had fallen asleep early and didn't get our call last night.

I'm hoping it means that she's not still upset.

But I really don't know what to expect.

As I shut off the car, the girls are already hopping out and running to Vanessa, who is waiting for us in the doorway. She's decked out in full equestrian wear. Sleek fitted black pants that mold her body, tucked into black riding boots. I look down at the jeans and flannel shirt I'm wearing.

"Are you a princess?" is the first thing out of Harlow's mouth. "Your house looks like Prince Eric's castle. Is there an ocean in the back?"

Vanessa laughs and gives her a hug. "I'm afraid I don't have an ocean, but I do have a pool."

"And horses, right? Daddy said we get to ride."

"Yes, I thought we'd start with that."

I greet Vanessa with a kiss on the cheek and can't help but wonder how this could ever possibly work. I feel a little like the pauper going into the princess's house.

I GET OVER myself and enjoy the beautiful day. We ride horses together and then the girls go for a swim. Afterwards, her chef helps them make their own pizzas.

"This is the best day ever," Harlow says, her mouth full of gooey cheese.

"I'm glad you're having fun," Vanessa says. She's gone out of her way to be nice to the girls, but she hasn't given me any clue as to how she's feeling about me. Part of me wonders if she's decided we should just be friends.

"What are we gonna do next?" Ava asks.

"We probably need to head home pretty soon," I tell them.

Vanessa grins at the girls. "What if we had a slumber party instead?"

"A slumber party! A slumber party!" they chant.

"Please, Daddy?" Harlow begs. "I swear it wasn't just the money. We really did want to see Miss Vanessa."

Vanessa glares at me with a raised eyebrow.

"I can explain," I say to her.

Shit.

"No, I can explain!" Harlow yells, wanting to be the center of attention. "So, silly Uncle Cam told us that if Daddy didn't use it, it was going to fall off."

"He was talking about his heart," Ava interrupts.

"Basically, my nosy brother paid the girls twenty dollars each to make sure that I hung out with you while they were here."

Vanessa laughs, thank god. And for the first time all day, I feel myself relax.

"I think I need to meet your Uncle Cam," she says to the girls.

"He's very silly," Harlow says. "Every time he sees me, he lifts me up in the air, turns me upside down, and shakes me to try and get the dimes to fall out of my pockets."

"Why do you have dimes in your pockets?"

"We play spoons for dimes when we're all together. Harlow wins a lot," Ava says.

"Your dad did invite me to meet your family for Thanksgiving. Should I bring dimes?" Vanessa asks.

"You probably better bring a lot, unless you are lucky like me," Harlow says, pointing to her chest.

"Okay, girls, why don't you take your plates into the

kitchen and put them in the dishwasher, then we'll get ready for bed."

"We don't have pajamas," Ava points out. "We only brought our swimsuits."

"Oh, I didn't think of that. Maybe you could borrow one of Vanessa's t-shirts." I turn toward Vanessa. Hell, she probably doesn't even own a t-shirt.

"I'm sure I can find something. Let me go look."

Once she is safely out of earshot, I say, "Girls, I know we're having a slumber party, but that doesn't mean you can stay up all night. It means you get to sleep here."

"So it's a sleepover, not a slumber party," Ava states. "There's a big difference."

"Yes, exactly. It's getting late and we've had a busy day. When I say it's time for bed, Harlow, that means you have to go to sleep, or we'll go home."

"Okay, Daddy," Harlow says. She gets up, washes her plate off and puts it in the dishwasher, showing me she means it.

"I found some T-shirts," Vanessa says, handing the girls shirts with movie posters for one of the *Trinity* movies on the front of them.

While they run into the bathroom to change, I take Vanessa into my arms.

"Thanks for today."

"I'm sorry I've been acting so crazy, Dawson. I don't have any excuse other than this is new to me. The way I feel about you. The way I already feel about them. The other day, when I left your office so suddenly, it was because . . ."

Harlow runs out of the bathroom. Make that, zooms out, pretending to be the airplane on the front of her shirt. She zooms down the hall and then zooms through the living room, her arms spread out wide.

"Harlow, don't run through the house, please," I say, interrupting Vanessa. Then I turn my attention back toward her. "You were saying you left my office the other day . . ."

CRASH!

I look up to see Harlow crashing into a small table and sending a very expensive looking vase flying through the air.

I let go of Vanessa and run, trying to catch it.

But I'm too late. It falls to the ground and shatters.

"I told you not to run in the house!" I yell.

"Harlow, you klutz!" Ava screams. "You're going to ruin *everything*! Vanessa will make us leave and Dad's heart will dry up and he'll die too! And then we'll be orphans!"

I stop in my tracks.

My children are afraid I'm going to die?

I take a deep breath and speak softly, wrapping both girls in a hug. "Ava, lower your voice. I'm not going to die. I'm not a dolphin." I turn toward Vanessa. "I'm sorry, we should probably go. We'll figure out a way to pay you for the vase."

Vanessa hasn't moved and I'm worried she's going to blow. Her body is still but her eyes are moving wildly across the room.

Harlow walks over to her with tears in her eyes. Her bottom lip is puffed out. "I'm very sorry."

Vanessa looks at Harlow like she just realized we're still here.

Then she bends down to Harlow's level and touches her hand. "It's okay, honey. There's a lot of breakable stuff here."

"I shouldn't have run in the house. I know better than that."

Vanessa smiles at her. "You know what. I think sometimes you need to run in the house. In fact, *I* feel like
running in the house." She takes off running. "Come on!"

The girls react first, quickly following her around the
kitchen islands. As they run by me, Vanessa grabs my shirt
and says, "You too."

I have no idea what Vanessa is doing, but I follow.

We run through her house and I realize we haven't even
seen half of it.

It's huge.

We run down hallways filled with rooms for entertain-
ment then around two bars, down a hall, around a pool
table.

Through a smoking lounge, den, and poker room.

A movie theater.

A dance floor.

Another lounge.

Then we run up a flight of stairs to a long hallway covered in deep plush carpet.

Down another long hall. Through bedrooms of different
colors.

Then Vanessa stops in front of a door at the end of a
hall.

She's breathing hard.

And just staring at the door.

She reaches out and touches the door's handle, almost
like she's afraid of it.

She finally turns the handle and throws open the door to
a giant playroom—filled with a multitude of toys and huge
stuffed animals.

"Whoa!" the girl say at the same time, their eyes big as
they run, skip, and jump from one thing to the next.

Vanessa still hasn't entered the room. She's just staring into it.

And I get the feeling that opening this door was like opening her heart.

I can't help but wonder if this room has something to do with the baby she lost.

"This is an amazing room."

She turns to me.

And I know by the look on her face and the tears in her eyes, that I'm right.

IT'S AMAZING THE pain another person can cause you.

Vanessa is tough. She's a strong business woman. Smart, beautiful, but she's as broken as I am.

And she just needs someone to love her.

To have the same hopes and dreams as her.

I think.

No, I'm going with my gut on this.

And I know I'm right.

I pull her into my arms and kiss her right in front of the girls.

"You want me to let go of the guilt, but you haven't, have you?"

She brushes away a tear, like she's mad it even dared to fall.

I move her hand away from her face, by pulling it to my lips and kissing it.

Then I look into her eyes and know that time doesn't matter.

It doesn't matter that we've only been together for a short time.

When you know it, you know it.

"I love you," I say.

"Now you're really going to make me cry," she says, smiling through her tears. "I love you too."

"I love you three! Harlow yells, running over and hugging both our legs.

"And I love you four," Ava adds, wrapping her arms around Vanessa.

Vanessa hugs her back tightly, tears now freely streaming down her face.

I usually hate to see tears.

With Whitney, tears were a bad thing.

The start of another bout of depression.

But these tears seem cleansing.

Freeing.

AFTER WE TUCK the girls into bed, I take Vanessa's hand and lead her out to the pool.

I stand in front of her. "Take your clothes off."

She looks surprised by this.

And normally, I'd want to undress her, but not now.

She needs this.

"Um," she says, looking puzzled.

"I'm taking my clothes off," I say as I strip them off and throw them into a chaise. "Get naked with me."

Her eyes trail hungrily down my body. I love the desire I see in them, but that's not what this is about.

If it were, I'd have her stripped and pinned under me in about two seconds flat.

I walk down the steps and into the pool, the water the perfect soothing temperature.

She takes her clothes off and joins me in the center.

"I don't like being told what to do," she says softly.

"I know you don't, but sometimes you need it." I give her a long, sweet kiss. Then I hold her shoulders, keeping her away from me. "You're naked," I state.

"Yeah, I am," she flirts.

"That means right here, in this pool, it's just us. Naked."

"You've said the word naked like four times. I get it. We're *naked*."

"We are physically, but I want you naked emotionally."

"What do you mean?"

"Tell me what happened. Why opening that playroom door hurt so bad. And why do you have a room like that?"

She takes a breath and slumps her shoulders, her body defeated.

I touch her face. "Tell me."

"I was pregnant. Almost four months along. I was happy. Bam was happy. We'd told everyone we knew. He wanted to start decorating the nursery, but I was afraid to. I'd had two other miscarriages. But they happened during the first trimester and once I got past that point, and got to see an ultrasound, I really got excited. I still was afraid to decorate the nursery, so I decided to do a playroom instead. I told myself when our friends with children visited, they would have a place to play. But, really, I was doing it for our future children. I bought all the stuff in the playroom. A few weeks later, I let myself start dreaming and thinking of names."

She starts tapping her foot.

I can tell this is the hard part.

"I started, um, losing the baby. Bam was out, supposedly at a business meeting. I called him when I was going to the hospital. He showed up about four hours later, after it was over, and I took one look at him and knew that he'd been cheating on me. There had been signs before, but he always reassured me. He said that I was silly and he loved me. Things would be amazing for a while. He could be amazing and attentive. He made me feel like a real life princess. Jewels the size of rocks, planes, yachts, traveling around the world, box seats, champagne. Whatever his heart desired. When you're little, you hear fairytales about princes and happily ever afters, but what you don't hear is that the prince is a spoiled brat who throws jewels and furs at you because he feels guilty for screwing around."

She keeps going, barely taking a breath. It's just rolling out of her.

"He admitted it that night. Said he loved me but that he's not a one-woman man. He tried to get me to understand that it should be okay. That the girls he did—and apparently there were many—meant nothing to him. That he loved me. I told him to get out. That I never wanted to see him again. The next day, as soon as I was released from the hospital, I filed divorce papers. I was on a mission. It drove me through the grief of losing the baby and the marriage."

I run my hands across her shoulders. My heart breaking for her.

"I shut my emotions off. Never cried. Never opened that door to the playroom . . ." She's been lost in her story, but she stops and looks into my eyes. "I haven't opened the playroom door since that day. Until tonight. It was so . . . freeing."

"I love you, Vanessa," I tell her. "And I swear I will never, ever cheat on you."

"I know you won't," she says. "In the office the other

day, I almost told you I loved you. I wasn't even thinking, it just came out. But I stopped myself because it seemed too soon."

"Vanessa, it's never too soon to tell someone how you feel."

"When you rightly wanted to spend time alone with your girls, it hurt me. More than it should have. And I felt stupid for letting you into my heart. I've been trying so hard to protect it."

I run my hands down the sides of her arms then entwine my hands with hers.

"We both have painful pasts. That's what this is about, letting go and opening up your heart to me. Telling me what you want. What you need."

"I want you to know what I need. I don't want to have to tell you," she says.

I pick her up and move us closer to the side of the pool, kissing her the whole time.

Her eyes fill up with tears again.

"Don't cry, baby. No more crying." I slowly kiss her wet cheeks, then her neck, then her lips. Taking my time. Showing her that with each kiss I want nothing more than to do just that.

But then she wraps her legs around my waist and deepens our kiss, her tongue tantalizing me, her curves flattened against me, her voice whispering my name.

"Dawson," she says.

And with one word, I know what she needs. It's the same thing I suddenly need. To be inside her.

I move my hands under her ass, lifting her toward me and causing her back to press against the side of the pool, as I pull her on top of me.

She leans her head back exposing her neck, so I take the opportunity to slide my tongue up its length, then rest my lips against hers.

Our lips are touching but not moving.

We're both perfectly still except for a gentle, occasional thrust of my hips.

I feel like I should come clean. Tell her the rest of my story. But it's not the right time. Not when she's clinging to me. Not when I finally feel the way I should feel.

Like I'm finally home.

Like I'm exactly where I belong.

She moves her lips against mine, kissing me slowly, then deepening the kiss while she grabs ahold of my ass.

I move faster, kissing her in time with my thrusts.

Until I can't kiss her any more.

She puts her lips on my shoulder, biting down slightly as she sighs with pleasure, and I feel my own release.

Then we're still again for a moment.

I bring my mouth to her ear and whisper to her. "You need me to take care of you and love you forever."

"That's exactly what I need," she replies, as I pick her up, carry her out of the pool and through the patio doors to her master bedroom.

I'm going to make love to her.

Slowly. Sweetly.

All night long.

EASTBROOKE ACADEMY – CONNECTICUT
ARIELA

I SUPPOSE IT'S sort of fitting that as I pull through

Eastbrooke's gates my dad calls me.

"Hi, Dad," I say into my phone.

"Ariela! Collin just told me what you're planning to do. I won't stand for it. You need to come home now and make this right. I can't even believe you would threaten both our livelihoods."

"I threatened Collin, Dad, because he threatened me. Not only does he cheat on me, but he tries to control me. I used to let him, but I'm not anymore. That goes for you too. And there's nothing either one of you can do about it."

"I'll side with Collin. Run your name through the mud. Disown you. You'll come out of your marriage with nothing."

"I don't care, Dad. I don't want *anything* from either one of you. I just want a divorce."

"Collin will be contesting the divorce, Ariela. If freedom is what you want, know it's the one thing you will never get."

"The hell you will," I hear my mother say loudly. "You will not take Collin's side on this."

I about drop the phone. I've never heard my mother raise her voice to my father.

"What the hell do you know?" my dad says to her. "It's not like you can do anything about it."

"Actually, I can. Ariela, dear, I'm putting you on speaker. I want you to hear this."

"Uh, okay . . ."

"I know you are probably too busy chasing skirts to pay much attention to the business," Mom says to my dad. "Luckily, I have been. And here's what I know. For years, your accountant has been signing portions of the business over to me for tax purposes."

"I'm fully aware of that," my dad says flatly. "Don't pretend like you know anything about my business."

"Oh, but I do. Because just last month, you signed over more."

"Yes, I know."

"I now own fifty-four percent."

"So?"

"So?" I hear papers slap his desk. "I'm divorcing you."

"You what? We have an agreement."

"Yes, but it's just a verbal one. I'm afraid those things don't stand up in court. I lied to you, darling. I've been lying through my teeth and looking the other way until I had control of your company. Just like you've lied to me about all the other women. Today is a happy day. Now, I need to get going soon. Going to meet a friend for a celebratory glass of champagne, but here's the deal. As long as neither you nor Collin contest your divorces then I won't fire either one of you. If you do, *poof*, you're gone. And Ariela, dear, I've heard that a lot of mothers and daughters are getting matching tattoos these days. I think we should get one after we get our matching divorces. And if you need anything, money, to talk, please call me."

"You can't do that!" my dad says angrily. I hear his chair push across the floor. "I'll fucking kill you first."

"Oh, dear. You shouldn't have said that. The police are waiting outside to escort you out of my house."

"Your house? This is *our* house."

"I'm afraid not. I also found out recently that the house has been in my name for the last seventeen years. You transferred it to me when the market tanked and you were worried you might lose your business. Apparently, you never bothered to transfer it back. You can pack up a few things while the nice policeman watches and then you will be escorted out. Have a nice life."

I hear a door slam and deep voice say, "Sir, you need to do as she asks."

Then click.

"Holy shit," I say to myself as I park.

My phone rings, this time it's my mom's cell phone.

"Mom! Holy hell! I can't believe you just did that. I'm so proud of you!"

"It's been a long time coming, Ariela. And I'm proud of me too. Where are you?"

"Believe it or not, I'm at Eastbrooke. It's Homecoming weekend."

"Are you there with Riley?"

"No. It's a long story, Mom."

"Tell me. Tell me everything that's happened since you left."

So I do. All of it.

"I THINK IT'S smart that you're there," she says. "You need to put the past behind you. It's been ten years. Even if you feel the same way about him, you're not the same girl you used to be."

"I still feel like that girl when I'm with him."

"Good luck, Ariela. I hope you work it out. And good luck with the event next week. I'm sure it will be amazing. If you're up for it, I'd like to visit you sometime."

"I'd like that too, Mom. Thanks for everything."

I get out of the car and walk down the sidewalk leading to the Student Center.

It's weird being back here.

As I walk by Hawthorne House, Riley's dorm, I stop to

touch a big red poster board megaphone that's covered with glitter and has the number twelve on it. Riley's number.

I remember how proud I was to wear his jersey before the big game. How it hung over my cheerleading skirt. How he said it was so sexy because it looked like it was all I had on.

Part of me wants to stop remembering. The memories both make me happy and make me hurt.

That's what I came here for, right? To see it all again. To let myself remember all the things I've been trying so hard to forget.

I wander down to the lacrosse field, knowing it's where I would end up.

Riley and I had come here together so many nights.

But one night, I came here alone.

I had just gotten back from a weekend at home.

My dad called me into his study, which was a shrine to the school we'd both worked so hard our whole lives to get me into.

He takes a photo off a shelf and hands it to me. "Do you remember the first time we visited?"

I study the photo. I'm decked out in Tiger gear and waving a pompom. "It was the first college football game I had ever been to."

"You were nine," my dad says. "We watched Princeton play Brown. I walked you around the campus and told you about my dream for you. Your mom and I didn't have much money when you were young, but we always put money into your college fund. And in a few weeks, you'll graduate Eastbrooke and then this fall you'll be there. Part of me can't believe it. This picture seems like it was yesterday."

"Um, Dad, I know you don't want to hear it, but I want to

go to USC with Riley. It's a really good school too."

"Ariela, I told you before, you're not going to California. You need to get that ridiculous notion out of your head."

A few months ago, I told my dad that I wanted to go to USC instead. He told me he wouldn't pay for anywhere but Princeton. When I got back to school and told Riley about it, he was pissed to learn that I had accepted to both USC and Princeton. He yelled at me and sped off in his car. But later, he showed up at my dorm and apologized. He shocked me when he got down on one knee and said Ariela, will you marry me, go to California with me, and love me forever? *I said yes and in a few weeks, I'll be on the beach saying* I do.

My dad takes the photo out of my hand and sits down next to me. "Are you really serious about not going to Princeton?" he asks.

"Yes, Dad. I'm sorry."

"Ariela, I know you think you love this boy now, but he's not worth ruining your future for. You have your whole life ahead of you. Princeton wasn't just my dream, it's been your goal. How many hours have you studied to maintain your grades just so you could get into Princeton?"

"A lot. I study a lot. But I love Riley."

"Riley is a boy. He can't take care of you. And if he promises you otherwise, he's lying to you."

"He has money. He said if you wouldn't pay for my college, he would."

"And what happens when you break up?"

"We're not going to break up."

My dad stares at me for a few seconds. Then he gets up and pulls a book off his shelf. "This is my high school yearbook." He opens it and starts pointing. "This is my high school girlfriend. We dated for three years. That's an eternity in high school relationships. We were voted most likely to get married. Best couple. We were prom king and queen. We broke up three months after graduation. Once high school was over, we had nothing in common anymore. No games or dances to go to. Our friends were off at different colleges. And our relationship died. And these two are Kelly and David, high school sweethearts who got married two weeks after graduation. They divorced a year later. And Patty and Bob. Couldn't keep their hands off each other. Broke up a week after graduation. My point is, high school relationships are like high school. They teach you about life and love. You're moving on to bigger and better things at Princeton. You'll meet the man of your dreams there. You'll go back there for Homecoming, not to Eastbrooke. Eastbrooke is just the stepping stone to the rest of your life. And so is Riley."

"No, he's not, Dad! He loves me and we're going to get married next week! I'm going to California. I'm eighteen. I'm an adult. And you can't stop me!"

"Getting married?" my dad says, sitting back in his chair, looking defeated. I'm sure my growing up is hard for him. I've always been such a Daddy's girl.

My dad rubs his hands down his face then looks at me and speaks in a very deep and serious tone. "You're right, Ariela. You are an adult. And you can choose whatever you want to do. But know your choices come with consequences. If you go to California, I know exactly what will happen. I know what boys like Riley are like. They've had life handed to them on a silver platter. They've never had to work a day in their life for anything. And when he gets to California, it's going to be full of beautiful women. Temptation. A boy like Riley is used to getting what he wants. And he'll take anything offered to him. And then, when he gets sick of you or moves on to the next thing, you'll be alone. You'll be broke and alone. And if that happens, don't come to me. It pains me more than anything to say this, because I've loved you your whole life. Your whole life, I've had nothing but your best interests in my heart. But if you make that choice, I'll disown you. Because I know in my heart that California is wrong for you. That you shouldn't give up your dream for a boy. And I'm so sure of my conviction, I'm willing to risk my relationship with my daughter, who I love more than life itself, on it. So, adult Ariela, it's up to you. Riley or your family."

He takes another picture down and sets it in my lap. Tears fill his eyes. I've never seen my dad cry before, and I realize how deeply I'm hurting him.

I look at the photo. I'm about four, wearing a princess costume, and I'm snuggled into my dad's arms asleep. You can see the love written all over my dad's face.

I sat here and pondered my life. My relationship with Riley. My future. I knew in my heart my dad only wanted the best for me. I knew in my soul that Riley loved me.

How do you choose between the man you've loved forever, your hero, your daddy, and the boy you're madly in love with?

I couldn't decide.

And it tore me apart.

I would come down here by myself just to cry.

And as the days to graduation ticked closer, the more sick I felt.

I wanted to tell Riley about my dilemma, but I couldn't bear to say the words. I couldn't admit to him that it was a difficult decision.

Just the thought of leaving him brought me to tears. I couldn't sleep, couldn't eat, couldn't study.

I'd look at my notebook, where I'd doodled *Mrs. Riley Johnson* across the top and start crying.

Riley consumed me. I'd never been in love like that before. Never loved someone so much. Never felt so much happiness. And, in my inexperience, I didn't understand that a love like that isn't replaceable. That if I left him, I'd never truly be happy again. Of course, I hoped he'd read my note and understand why I had to go to Princeton. But he never got my note. And I didn't realize it until it was too late.

If there's one moment in my life I wish I could take back and do over, it's the moment I told him I was going to Princeton.

I tried to forget Riley.

I tried to move on, but spent most of my summer in tears.

If it weren't for Collin, I don't know that I would have made it. He was there. Told me everything I needed to hear and made me believe I did the right thing.

But I'd still cry myself to sleep. The ache in my heart so deep.

About six months later, I looked up Riley's profile. His cover photo was all of them on the beach. Aiden and Keatyn, Brooklyn and his girlfriend, Maggie and Logan, Dallas and RiAnne, and Riley with his arm wrapped around a gorgeous blonde in a skimpy bikini. His profile picture was him under the Hollywood sign, wearing sunglasses and holding his arms out wide—like he had made it. He looked happy. He was fine without me. I started to wonder if my dad was right. If we wouldn't have lasted anyway.

The next day I told Collin we could make it official. I would be his girlfriend.

But then when my wedding came . . .

"Ariela? Is that you?" I hear Riley's voice.

"What are you doing here?"

"What are you doing here?" he asks me.

"I'm remembering, Riley."

"Me too," he says somberly. "I'm sorry."

"You're sorry?"

"Yeah. Looking back, there are a lot of things I should have done differently. I shouldn't have expected you to give up your dream of going to Princeton. I shouldn't have assumed you could just ditch your family—go against their wishes—to come with me. I was cocky and selfish. But god, Ariela, I loved you. All I could think about was being with you. Always. I thought we'd get married and live happily ever after. It all caught me so off guard. If you would've just talked to me."

"I tried."

"That's the thing, Ariela. I don't remember you trying. Did I just not want to hear it? Did I dismiss it?"

"No, I couldn't do it. Couldn't even bring myself to say it."

"I knew something was bothering you. I asked you if you were okay. You weren't eating."

"I was a wreck inside. I was overwhelmed."

"And I thought I had everything figured out."

I smile at him and chuckle. "You've never lacked for confidence, Riley."

"I didn't tell you the complete truth before when you asked why I'm here. I'm not just remembering, Ariela. I think I'm healing."

"You are? How? I thought I'd come here and get closure, but I'm not. It's not closing anything. It's like it's opening me back up. My heart. My mistakes. It all feels so fresh here."

"And painful," he says.

"Yes."

He opens his arms and I fall into them.

He holds me close and whispers, "How long have you been here?"

"About an hour."

"Where else have you been?"

"Just here, Riley. This is the first place I came. It's where we'd dream. Remember how we'd lay on a blanket, look at the stars, and plan our future? The future I ruined."

"I got here last night. The first place I went was the spot under the tree outside the auditorium."

Tears fill my eyes. "Oh, Riley."

"Yeah. But then we went to the game. And there was this cheerleader who had the number twelve on her face. And then, I don't know, something changed. I started remembering all the fun we had. Not just you and me, but all of us. At Stockton's. At lunch. At The Cave. Dances. I had turned off all the good memories because they were too painful. But here, I was overloaded with them. Everywhere I turned, a memory. And tonight I realized something. It wasn't just your fault. So I'm letting it all go. I forgive you, Ariela."

I grab his shirt and start sobbing.

Sobbing like I did the second I got in the car. Where he couldn't see me. I cried harder than I ever have in my life.

Riley holds me tighter, and when I feel his chest heave, I know he's crying too.

After a few minutes he kisses the top of my head then pushes up my chin.

"You know what you need, Ariela Ross? A trip down

memory lane. Come with me and let's remember the good stuff."

"Then what?"

"Then, we're going to party at Stockton's like old times. Keatyn wants me to see our class gifts."

"Gifts?"

"I guess they decided to do two years since technically we had it for that long."

EASTBROOKE ACADEMY — CONNECTICUT
RILEY

I GRAB HER hand and lead her up the hill. When we get to the soccer pitch, I say, "Remember when we won our playoff game?"

"I remember the whole team taking their shirts off. I remember thinking you looked so cute. I always loved your shoulders. They seemed so strong. Like nothing bad could happen if I was with you."

"I remember you running down the bleachers, jumping into my arms, and kissing me."

"I remember that too. You were sweaty."

"What about after?"

"We partied at Stockton's, of course, but then we snuck off. I brought you down here on the field."

"And had your way with me," I laugh.

"Yes, I did. You seemed to like it," she says.

"I always liked it with you, Ariela." I drag her away from the soccer field and toward the field house.

"Do you remember sneaking me into the cheerleading locker room?"

She swats me. "I still can't believe you talked me into it. We could have gotten expelled."

"The things we did surrounded by pompoms," I joke.

"This trip down memory lane seems to be us remembering all the sex we had."

I squeeze her hand. "You and I both know it was more than just sex. We had fun, Ariela. I remember you laying all the pompoms on the floor giggling at the thought of us doing it there. I remember the way your bangs would hang over your right eye and you'd always be pushing it back behind your ear. I remember how soft your skin was. The way your laughter was like music. That shy smile you'd give me when we were about to do something risky."

"Speaking of risky," she says, pointing toward Hawthorne House. "Thank goodness you got a first floor room your senior year and I could just sneak in the window. I used to be so nervous sneaking in there at night. Of course, that just added to the excitement. Being with you always felt a little dangerous."

"I will forever be the boy who ruined Ariela Ross' reputation for perfection."

"You did make me get a B on a test once. You were a bad study partner."

"Me?" I ask, holding my hand to my chest. "I kissed you for every right answer."

"Which meant we only got through about a quarter of the flashcards before those kisses turned into more."

"I loved your cheerleading skirt."

"What's that got to do with studying?" she asks.

"I was supposed to be studying with Dallas one night in the library, but I knew you were in the gym working on posters for the pep rally. So we skipped studying and came to help you. You had on your practice skirt and kept bending over to pick stuff up. It was the perfect tease."

"Do you remember when I came and helped you and Keatyn make signs, before we were dating? You wrote your name on my arm in glue then covered it in glitter. I didn't wash my arm for days."

Our phones buzz at the same time.

"Text from Keatyn," I say, pulling it out of my pocket and looking at it.

"Me too," she says. "Maggie must have told her I was here."

"It says we're supposed to go to Stockton's now."

"But it's still early," she says.

"Probably pre-partying."

"Do you still have a key?"

Our phones buzz again.

I look at mine. "Another text from Keatyn. It says they will meet us there, but if we get there first to just use our thumbs."

"Thumbs?"

I shrug. "No idea."

We head to the chapel. "I used to come to church all hungover on Sunday mornings just to hear you sing."

"You were sweet," she says, taking my hand and pulling me down the back hall, down the stone steps, then down a narrow hall filled with meeting rooms and crypts of those long since passed.

When we get to the familiar one of Mary Jane Stockton, we pass it, continuing toward what appears to be a dead end in front of us. We slip behind an unseen narrow gap between the dead end and the stone wall, take twenty steps around a corner, then I shine my phone toward what appears to be the side of a crypt. I flip open the seventh fleur-de-lis.

"The keyhole is gone," Ariela says.

I examine it closer, moving my flashlight across it. "Look, it's been replaced with glass and underneath the glass is a small etching that says Class of 2004."

"Keatyn said to use our thumb. Put your thumb on the glass."

"Biometrics? Wow. That was a cool class gift."

"Beats using a key. Especially when you're trying to hurry."

I open the door and look at Eastbrooke's elite's party place, Stockton's. Each year, one student is given a key and a great responsibility. The key is passed down to those who are deemed worthy. My older brother, Camden, gave it to me in our junior year.

"Look!" Ariela says. "There's a furry rug!"

Our phones buzz again.

Keatyn: *You have a half hour alone. Use it wisely.*

"I almost broke up with you over a furry rug," she says. "Remember when Dallas asked Kassidy to formal with the furry rug from your room because they'd had sex on it?"

"Yeah, that asshole. I almost killed him for that. That was our rug."

"You know, it wasn't until I saw the movie that I realized why you even had a girly green furry rug in your room. It was sweet of you to sleep on Keatyn's floor during Homecoming because you were afraid she was in danger."

"I told her I was having a hot affair with her rug, so she gave it to me. And then one night you and I made out on it and, from that point on, all I could think about was doing you on it. Do you remember our first time?" I grab her hand and pull her toward the rug.

"Yeah, I was so nervous. It's not like I hadn't done it before but—"

"It was the first time it really meant something," I say, finishing her sentence.

"I made you wait a long time."

"Fifty-four days."

"You remember how many days?" she says, a surprised smile forming on her face.

"Yeah. It was torture."

"I suppose I was sort of purposely torturing you." She grins. "You had a reputation for loving them and leaving them."

"Still do," I say with a laugh.

"Was there ever anyone serious?"

"I didn't sleep with anyone for six months after our graduation."

"Really?" She closes her eyes. "Oh, Riley. Is it bad that makes me feel good?"

"Why does it make you feel good?"

"My dad said I was a passing fancy."

"You weren't. Obviously. Now, I have a strict seventy-two hour rule. Once I hit that with the same girl, it's time to move on. No feelings. No pain. You didn't tell me you married Collin. Remember when I punched him? Your parents were pissed. That's when they started on you, isn't it?"

She nods. "They said you were impulsive."

"I was! Still am, actually." I grab her face and kiss her, laying her back on the rug.

When she opens her eyes, she says, "Oh, Riley! Look at the twinkle lights on the ceiling! Aiden and Keatyn always had a thing for stars."

"Makes you feel like you're at The Cave when you are inside and warm."

"Look, in the corner. Spelled out with stars. *Class of 2004.* That's us too."

I get up and pull her to her feet. "Let's look at our names. Remember when we wrote them here? We used Keatyn's Thanksgiving toast, which started a trend of putting our names together on the wall. Like the founders did."

"Here are the founder's names!" she says, running her hand across the top of the inscription as I read it.

> *"All who enter Stockton's grotto*
> *Swear to uphold our ultimate motto*
> *Never speak of its location*
> *Or risk a life of eternal damnation*
> *For this is a place of legend and lore,*
> *So, party on, friends,*
> *Evermore.*

Stanford Thacker III
Olivia Carder
Karoline Talbot
Oliver Nasbith
Class of 1972."

"And here are ours!" she says.

"We can only be said to be alive in those moments
when our hearts are conscious of our treasures.
(Thorton Wilder)

Riley Johnson
Ariela Ross
Aiden Arrington
Keatyn Douglas
Dallas McMahon
Logan Pedersen
Maggie Morgan
Class of 2004. *"*

While she's reading, I'm remembering the day we signed it.

"I'm first! I'm the one who got the key," I say, grabbing the marker from Keatyn after she writes our class quote on the wall.

I sign my name and then joke with Ariela as she writes her name in hot pink.

"You should just write Ariela Johnson, since that's what it will be soon."

"The L in your name overlaps the Y in mine. I remember thinking when we signed it that we'd be tied together forever. It's weird coming back here and not being together."

"Yeah, it is," she agrees.

"I remember exactly what you looked like that day. Your smile was bright. There was a bounce in your step. You were wearing my Eastbrooke athletics sweatshirt that was way too big on you. Sometimes you'd wear it without a bra and I couldn't wait to sneak my hands up it."

"You snuck your hands up it regardless of what was underneath, Riley." She pauses and just looks into my eyes. "Thanks for tonight. I think I pushed all the memories of us deep down inside because they were painful. Now, they don't feel that way. They're just good memories. I know everyone will be here soon, so I just want to tell you that I remember what you said to me that night on the balcony. I don't want to cause you anymore pain, Riley. The wedding is next week. If you still want me gone, I'll leave after it and stay out of all your lives."

"I have a really busy week coming up," I tell her.

"And I'll be onsite at the vineyard."

"That's probably good. It will give us both time to think about what we really want. So, at the wedding. We'll decide. Together."

"Either way, you have to promise you'll dance with me," she says.

"I'll dance with you right now."

I dim the lights, hook up my iPhone to the wall speaker from the Class of 2013 and hit a playlist I've transferred to every iPod and phone I've owned in the past ten years.

"Riley," she says, facing me, standing under the twinkle lights. "That's . . . That's our song."

"Actually, it's our playlist."

"You still have it?" She puts her hand over her heart.

"I do, but I haven't listened to it since the last time we danced together. Remember, in my room, the night before graduation? You cried. The whole time. I could feel your tears on my shoulder. I just thought you were sad because it was our last night in my dorm. Had I known it would be our last time ever—"

"Our last time ripped my heart out," she says, tears filling her eyes again as I sweep her into my arms and dance with her.

"You held me so tight. How did you end up back with Collin?"

"He was there when I was upset. Princeton was . . . Complicated for me. My parents were thrilled I was there. When my dad helped me move into my dorm, he said it was the proudest day of his life. For me, it felt empty. I felt empty without you. And you never called me. I thought that you would, but I understand why you didn't. Anyway, Collin got me out of my dorm, talked me into getting involved on campus. It was easier to just do it than explain my feelings. He was nice, but he was never you."

"You married him."

"I almost didn't."

"What do you mean?"

"Before the wedding, I called you. I was having a panic attack and didn't think I could go through with it. I had decided that if you answered I wouldn't marry Collin and that if you didn't it was a sign that I should."

"I didn't answer."

"You didn't answer," she says sadly.

"It was six years ago. A Saturday afternoon in June," I tell her. "I had just finished golfing. When your name flashed across the screen my heart stopped. I froze."

"Do you remember in the movie how Keatyn's grandpa told her to flip a coin and she'd know what she wanted? I knew what I wanted and it wasn't Collin. But you didn't answer, so I thought fate was telling me something. And my dad told me it was just cold feet. That Collin was perfect for me. And I felt bad because they had spent so much on the wedding."

"After I made my first million, I used to imagine going to your house and telling your dad he was wrong about me. When you came back into my life, I imagined a similar scenario. But then I went to pick you up and saw you kissing him . . ."

"I didn't know he was coming. When I opened the door, I was expecting you."

"Why did you kiss him?"

"He kissed me. I'm assuming you didn't stay long enough to see me push him away?"

I hang my head. "No, I didn't. I was . . ."

"Understandably upset," she says. "I'm sorry. And thank you for the flowers. They were beautiful."

"Your favorite. Remember when I promised to be a good husband?"

"You told me you'd bring me flowers every week. We thought it was so simple then, Riley. I've got to be honest with you. I'm not the same girl anymore. Life has left me feeling jaded and unhappy. I've been weak. I've let my life play out instead of living it. I've been going through the motions. And I take full responsibility for my actions. I'm ready to move on. Or start over. I didn't know if I was just romanticizing the past when I went to California. I just knew I had to go. For the first time in my life, I truly felt like I knew what I was supposed to do. Where I was supposed to be. I can't tell you how both freeing and terrifying it felt. But then the other night when we made love, all those feelings I had been pushing deep down resurfaced and I knew I made the right choice. We know the chemistry is still there between us. We know the feelings are still there. We need to see if the love is still there. And if we like the people we've become."

"So we need to start over. Sort of."

"I think so. I also need to tell you something else. Something I should have told you long before now. On graduation day, when we ran into each other outside the auditorium and I told you, I was going to put a note on your car. I wasn't going to tell you in person. But there you were."

She reaches in her pocket and pulls out a worn looking folded up piece of paper. She lays it in my hand just as there's a knock on the door.

"I think our time is up." I hand the note back to her.

"You keep it, Riley. Maybe read it sometime. It says everything I wanted you to know that day but couldn't say."

I give her a sad smile and shove the note in my pocket as the door opens and about thirty former Stockton's members stroll in.

Keatyn and Dallas are the last ones to enter.

"We held them off as long as we could." She looks at me tentatively.

I wrap one arm around Ariela and the other around her and, just like I used to, say, "It's time to party."

Dallas joins our group hug. "You girls getting up on the bar to dance, for old times sake?"

"Hell yes," both Keatyn and Ariela say then go running up to the bar.

As Dallas and I watch them dance with some other girls they've coaxed up with them, he says, "Why did she come? Did she know you were here?"

"She came for the same reason I did. To put the past behind her."

Sunday, October 12th

HOTEL SUITE – CONNECTICUT
GRACIE

"YOU MADE HOMECOMING amazing," Baylor tells me as he drops me off at the hotel suite. "I'm so glad you surprised me."

"Even though it caused you some girl trouble?" I tease. My back is against the door, my chin raised. I've been hoping all night that he'd kiss me already.

He touches my cheek. "You have a little bruise."

"I have a magazine cover shoot tomorrow."

"What will you tell them?"

"That I got in a wicked cat fight over an adorable boy."

"You think I'm adorable?" he asks, his lips moving closer. "Girls don't usually say that about me."

"I wouldn't be here if I didn't think that. What do they usually say?"

He shrugs, looks shy. "I don't know."

"I know what they say, Baylor. They say you're hot. You're a Hawthorne. You're an amazing quarterback. You drive an expensive car. I hear the same things. She's hot.

She's Tommy Steven's and Abby Johnston's daughter. She's rich. She was nominated for an Academy Award. She blah blah blah. They say things that aren't so nice too. I think you're adorable because you were a gentleman who offered me his seat. Because you send me texts that actually have substance and not just ask me what's up. Because you opened the car door for me. Because you asked my sister what my favorite color was and then went out and bought me flowers. And because I loved the way you held me when we danced."

He grabs my face and kisses me. Unexpectedly hard. I wrap my arms around his neck and kiss him back just as hard. So hard I don't have time to breathe. Or maybe it's that the kiss took my breath away.

"Wow," I say, when he ends the kiss and looks into my eyes.

"The perfect ending to the perfect night," he says. "Goodbye, Gracie."

"Goodbye," I say sadly, not wanting him to leave.

"You look sad," he says. "You come to Eastbrooke and there will be a lot more of those."

"And if I can't?"

"I may decide to go to school in California," he says with a grin then he pushes my chin up with his finger and gives me one more kiss before he leaves.

I WALK INTO the suite and flop on the bed next to Keatyn in a happy daze.

"How was your night?" she asks.

"Amazing. I really see why you loved it here."

"So, do you like Eastbrooke or do you like Baylor?"

"Both."

"If you decide to give up acting and go to school, don't do it for a boy, Gracie. Do it for yourself."

"When I visited, Keatyn, I did it because I wanted to. Not because of a boy. I didn't know at the time that Brady would sleep with Kylie and I didn't know I would meet Baylor. You're the reason I've been thinking about it."

"I am?"

"Not just you, but all of you. Maggie, Riley, Dallas. You have amazing friends. Even before Kylie hooked up with Brady, I knew she wasn't the same kind of friend. I don't have any friends."

"You don't? What about Dylan and Tabitha? You grew up together on *The Gracie Experiment*."

"We were best friends on set, but then as soon as I quit and went on to do movies, they sort of stopped being my friends."

"They haven't really gone on to do anything else, have they?"

"Dylan does some commercials, but that's about it. Do you think that's why? It's like they decided they don't like me anymore."

"Sometimes that happens in this business."

"I heard them talking behind my back one time. About how I only got to switch to movies because of who I am. That I'm not even that good of an actress."

"Well, obviously you are. You were nominated for an Academy Award already. That's pretty unusual and not something they give out just because you're related to someone famous. Your dad's never been nominated."

"I know. He told me that. It's a hard choice. I love acting. It's always been something I felt compelled to do."

"You used to do shows for us when you were little," she

says. "You would make Pooh dance. And you wanted to rename him Mr. Bear because he didn't want to be named after poop."

"I've seen the videos. Pretty funny, huh?"

"Well, it just shows that you've been working on your craft for a long time. Not to mention the acting lessons you take too."

"I want to keep getting better, but I also wish I could just be normal."

"Just because you're famous doesn't mean you can't be normal. You act in public. You're yourself in private."

"Maybe that's the problem. In public, I am myself."

"It's up to you to decide what you want the world to see. For example, there are no photos of you and Baylor on your Instagram."

"And there won't be."

"Why?"

I touch my lips. "Because I want to keep him to myself."

"Did you kiss him?"

"He kissed me goodnight."

"And?"

"It was an amazing kiss. I didn't think he was going to kiss me. He held my hand all night. We danced and had so much fun. And I like his friends. They're fun too. We had a lot of fun at the after party. Danced our asses off."

"I bet you're tired," she says, pulling a throw over me.

"I wasn't until I laid down."

"Are you flying back home with us?"

"No, I have a cover shoot in New York tomorrow."

"Who are you staying with? How are you getting there?"

"You know Mom and Dad won't let me travel without my bodyguard, Cooper Junior."

"Yet, you ditched him and came here by yourself," she scolds.

"He told me Tommy yelled at him. He's meeting me here at noon then a car is driving us into the city. Dad's going to be in town shooting a commercial, so we're staying with him."

"Will you get into trouble?"

"They maybe kinda think you invited me. Does Mom know you didn't?"

"I didn't tell her, no," she says with a smile.

I give her a hug. "You're my favorite sister."

"Get some sleep, Gracie."

"Or I could tell you about the kiss."

She perks up. "You could."

I sit up and face her. I can't help it. I'm so freaking excited, so I tell her every single detail of my amazing night.

HOTEL SUITE – CONNECTICUT
RILEY

"WE'VE GOT TO go!" Dallas yells, waking me out of a deep sleep.

"What's wrong?"

"RiAnne is in labor," he says, his phone up to his ear. "For real this time. We've got to get that pretty little jet of yours in the air." He says into his phone, "Okay, baby. Hang on." Then he turns to me. "She wants to talk to you."

I shake my head no, but he puts the phone to my ear anyway.

"Hey, RiAnne," I mumble, my voice not working this early.

"If I have this baby alone, Riley, there will be hell to pay. Please—Oh, shit, that hurts—hurry!"

I hop out of bed and start throwing clothes in my bag. "Did you get Keatyn and Gracie up?"

"Gracie's getting picked up at noon. And Keatyn's up," he says. I run in the bathroom to grab the rest of my things and can hear him still talking.

"Baby, it's okay. Calm down. Worse case, I'll video conference."

I can't hear what she says but I can hear her yelling. I don't think she wants to video conference the birth with him.

"Just tell the baby he needs to wait until Daddy gets there," Dallas says calmly. I really don't know how the hell he's so calm. I'm a nervous wreck. It's my fault that he's here in the first place. I'll be damned if he's going to miss his baby being born because of me.

"I'm ready," I say, rolling my bag out of the room with Dallas in tow.

"Are you ready, Keatyn? We've got to go now!"

"Have you called the pilot?" Keatyn asks me.

"Shit! No!"

Dallas covers his phone. "He's the first person I called."

"How are you so damn calm?" I ask him.

"Baby number five, I suppose."

He grabs Keatyn's tote, gives Gracie a kiss goodbye, and we head out.

The elevator feels like it takes forever. *Come on.*

Keatyn leans her head on my shoulder. "I think I'm still asleep."

I wrap my arm around her, imagining Aiden will not be as calm as Dallas when it comes time to have their baby.

"You can sleep on the plane."

Dallas is still talking to RiAnne. "We'll be wheels up in twenty minutes. Six hours I'll be there, if not sooner. I know. I know." He turns to me. "Ri says that she hates you right now."

Keatyn grabs the phone from Dallas. "Hey, Ri. How you doing? Just think. This is the last time that you'll ever be in labor. Your last baby. Slow down and enjoy it if you can."

I hear more yelling.

"Uh, okay. Um, does it help to know that Dallas bought you something spectacular for this one? Since it's the last."

She hands the phone back to Dallas.

"Yes, of course I did. It's our last baby. You've been an amazing mother and are my beautiful Pookiebear. Spectacular is an understatement."

VANESSA'S ESTATE – HOLMBY HILLS
DAWSON

I WAKE UP to find sunlight streaming through the windows and Vanessa gone from her bed.

I look at the clock, shocked it's almost nine and immediately worried about the girls.

I quickly get dressed and follow the chatter out to the kitchen.

Vanessa and the girls are making pancakes together. Their conversation is loud and animated. They are chatting happily about their grandma and grandpa's beach house. How Daddy's toe got bit by a crab.

Vanessa's hair is pulled back off her face, and she's wearing my shirt with a pair of jean shorts.

Her long legs are tan and her feet are bare.

For a few precious moments, I just observe.

Scenes like this never happened at our home. Whitney didn't like to eat breakfast and was rarely up in time. The medication that she took made her sleep hard through the night.

But since we moved in with my parents, making breakfast together has become a happy new ritual for me and the girls.

I want to rush to Vanessa and hug her for starting without me.

She has no idea how much this means to me.

I suppose, eventually, I'm going to have to get naked too. Tell Vanessa the whole truth about what happened with Whitney. But I'm afraid if I do . . .

"Daddy!" Harlow yells.

She runs and jumps into my arms, so I pick her up and carry her back to the island.

"We're making pancakes," Ava says, looking up from the batter she's stirring.

"The girls and I have made a decision," Vanessa says.

"What's that?"

"We decided that this house is too stuffy. There are too many things that are breakable and I'm getting rid of it. Selling it. Starting over."

I set Harlow on the counter, kiss the top of Ava's head, and then pull Vanessa into my arms.

"It's a gorgeous house. The architecture, the location, the grounds. Maybe what it needs is a new look. A little remodeling to turn it into something that's more you."

"More me?"

"Yeah, like the you today. Who even knew Vanessa

Flanning owned a pair of cutoffs."

She looks down at herself and smiles. Then she looks around the room and at my daughters.

"You're doing a great job, Ava," Vanessa says. "Go ahead and pour them onto the griddle."

"No! Daddy has to do that part," Harlow objects. "The griddle is hot!"

"I think Ava is old enough to be careful. What do you think, Ave? Can you handle it?"

She beams. "Oh course I can! I've been telling you for years that I'm old enough."

"What can I do?" Harlow pouts.

"Why don't you help me heat up the syrup?" Vanessa says to her.

While they work on the syrup, Ava says, "Will you teach me how to flip them, Dad? I know I need to watch for the bubbles, but I'm afraid that I'll ruin them."

"You can't ruin pancakes, sweetie. But why don't I hold your hand while you do the first one?"

She nods and I hold her hand on top of the turner. We gently slide it under the pancake then carefully flip it.

"We did it!" she says, excitedly.

"Now, you do the rest."

"Oh, shoot. I messed that one up a little, but look!"

"You are officially the new pancake maker. Now I can sleep in late."

"No way. Pancake making is fun because we're all together."

AFTER WE'VE DEMOLISHED the pancakes, the girls head up to the playroom.

"Thank you," Vanessa says to me, as she's clearing dishes.

"For what?"

"For this morning. Sharing your girls with me. This is what I always dreamed of, a house full of kids."

"Have you ever thought of adopting?"

"I've thought of a lot of things. I just kept thinking— never mind, it's silly."

I pull her into my arms. "Tell me."

"I was hoping there'd be a father in the picture. Would you want more kids?"

"Yes. But not yet."

"Oh."

"Not until—"

"Until what?"

"Until I get married again."

"Oh," she says, a grin creeping across her face.

"Come here," I say, guiding her lips toward mine.

CEDARS-SINAI MEDICAL CENTER — LOS ANGELES
KEATYN

WE MAKE IT to the hospital just in time. Dallas runs to get scrubbed in and Riley and I collapse in the private waiting room.

I reach out and grab his hand. "You're a good friend and pretty freaking brilliant. What made you think of the helicopter?"

"It was my pilot's idea. I just agreed to pay for it."

"Well, it was smart. If we would've had to go through traffic, we wouldn't have made it."

"How was Homecoming?" Aiden asks, joining us and greeting me with a kiss.

"It was good," Riley says. "Thanks for letting her come with me."

He laughs and squeezes my hand. "Somehow I don't think I had a say in it."

"She is pretty stubborn," Riley teases. "But it was good. Ariela was there. We talked. Partied together. And decided to think about things this week. We're deciding at the wedding if we want to try again or not."

"At *my wedding*?? Oh, no, you're not!" I say.

"Why not?"

"Because it's supposed to be a happy occasion! Don't make her leave the wedding, Riley."

"I'm not going to make her leave. We just don't know if we should try again. We aren't the same people we were back in high school."

"I think that's a good thing," Aiden states.

"Why do you think that?" Riley asks him.

"Because you've grown up a lot. You've lived a lot. You've had a lot of life experiences. If things do work out for the two of you this time, you will appreciate it more. You'll cherish it."

Dallas steps into the room. "Ready to meet the newest McMahon?"

I'm the first to react, jumping up before the guys.

Aiden takes my hand and we follow Dallas into their room.

RiAnne is sitting up in bed, holding a little pink bundle.

"It's a girl!?" I screech. "You were so sure it was a boy!"

"I know!" RiAnne says, happily. "We're so glad we didn't find out. It was a very fun surprise."

I slather on hand sanitizer and then gently touch the baby's cheek. "Look at her. Oh, RiAnne, she's so beautiful."

"You are, aren't you?" Dallas says, nestling the bundle in his arms and continuing to talk to it. "Carder put your Mommy through ten hours of labor. And your sister, Fallon, twenty hours. So, you're already our favorite."

He hands the bundle off to me and I notice that he discreetly takes a box from Aiden.

"Thanks for picking it up, man," he says, giving Aiden a guy hug.

"Congratulations," Aiden says back. "You're a blessed man."

"That I am," Dallas says, returning to RiAnne's side and taking her hand.

Aiden sits next to me and caresses the baby's cheek while I unwrap the cocoon of blankets.

"Look at her little chubby cheeks," he says. "They're so perfectly pink."

"And look at her hands," I say. "They're so dainty. Ri, did you decide on a name?"

"I think we should go with Farryn," RiAnne says to Dallas. "That was your favorite, right?"

He kisses her hand and looks into her eyes. "You're my favorite," he says sweetly to her.

RiAnne looks toward the baby and gets teary eyed. "We're so lucky. It's hard to believe my getting pregnant and us getting married so young turned out like it did."

"No, it's not," Dallas says. "I knew this is exactly how we'd be. Happy. With a mess of kids. And I was thinking . . ."

"About what?" she asks.

"Our wedding."

"Our wedding was a bit of a disaster," she says with a laugh. "Remember how the wind picked up and almost blew the altar over?"

"I remember the groom was pretty hung over," Riley says.

"So were the groomsmen," Aiden adds with a laugh.

"It was still beautiful," I say. "You were both so in love that the weather didn't matter."

"I think we should do it again," Dallas says seriously.

"Do what again?" RiAnne asks.

"Get married. What would you think of doing it up right? Renewing our vows? Having a killer reception. We have a lot to celebrate in our life. Five beautiful, healthy children. We're still in love. I know you hated being pregnant, especially this time, but this, this moment right here makes all that bitching worthwhile. Look at her. Ten perfect toes. Ten perfect fingers. And this one isn't a cone head."

"Dallas!" she chastises but then he puts the box Aiden just handed him in front of her and opens it. RiAnne's eyes practically bug out of her head.

"Son of a biscuit!" she says. "Is that for me?"

"Yes," Dallas says, taking her hand, slipping off her wedding ring, and putting the new ring on her. "This one has five rows of diamonds for our five children."

"And the huge diamond in the middle?" she asks.

He takes her face in his hands. "That one's for us. Will you marry me again?"

"Ohmigawd, Dallas. Yes. Yes."

Then she says, "Keatyn, holy shit, come look at this!"

I hand the baby off to Aiden, who pulls her close to his broad chest, causing my heart to swell. I can only imagine what it will feel like when he's holding our own little bundle of joy in his strong arms. His smile will be on perma-blaze.

I go to the side of RiAnne's bed and *ooh* and *aah* over her ring, but I can't stop sneaking peeks at Aiden. He has on an pale green oxford shirt that plays off his beautiful green eyes. His sleeves are rolled up showing off strong forearms that look perfect with a baby in them. I laugh to myself thinking about what Katie said about Knox. That he would make her ovaries explode. That's how I feel when I look at Aiden, only my heart feels like it could explode with joy. I touch my own little baby bump and smile.

AFTER A LITTLE bit, a nurse comes in and shoos us out, saying the mother and baby need their rest.

"What are you doing now?" Aiden asks Riley.

"No plans, really," he says.

"I bought some steaks. Thought we could grill out."

"Marvel's night off, huh?"

"It is."

"You know what?" Riley says. "I think I'm going to take a rain check. I'm going home. This weekend has given me a lot to think about."

"Are they happy thoughts?" I ask, giving him a kiss on the cheek goodbye.

"They are. In fact, when I get home, I'm going to call Ariela. I actually can't wait to talk to her. We used to talk on the phone for hours. Sometimes we'd fall asleep talking to each other. It always amazed me how we never ran out of things to talk about. And now we have ten years of things to talk about."

"I think that's awesome," I say, smiling at him.

"And I second the awesome motion," Aiden says. "You

seem happy. Is it because of the baby or because of the weekend?"

"I'm happy for Dallas and RiAnne, but I'm also happy for me. I'm lucky to have friends who care enough about me to force me to face something I didn't want to face. And she showed up there too. I'd say that was fate."

"I'd say it was fate too," I say, feeling so happy for all my friends today.

IN THE CAR – L.A.
RILEY

I DON'T WAIT until I get home to call her. I do it the minute I get in the car that picks me up.

"Riley," she says, her voice causing my heart to flutter. "Are you back in L.A. already?"

"I am. RiAnne called this morning in a panic because she was in labor, so we left in a hurry. How was your early morning flight?"

"I can't believe I went straight from the party to the airport, but it was good. I slept the whole way. So, how's RiAnne? Did they have the baby yet?"

"They did. We got there just in time. And they had a beautiful baby girl. Farryn."

"Aww, that's a pretty name. Remember when we named our future children?"

"Yeah, you liked Madison and Katelyn for our girls," I say.

"And you liked Dylan and Noah for our boys," she says then starts laughing. "I don't think I'd want to use those names now."

I laugh too. "Me either. So what are you doing today?"

"I just printed off my massive checklist for the wedding and am going to start running through everything in my head to make sure I'm not missing any details. Details are what make the difference between a nice wedding and a perfect wedding."

"I bet. I had fun last night, Ariela."

"I did too, Riley."

"Remember how we used to talk on the phone for hours?"

"Sometimes we'd even fall asleep talking."

"I was thinking maybe we could do that this week. Talk. Every night. I want to know what you've been doing the last ten years. I want to tell you about my business. My plans. I want to know what your dreams are. What's on your life bucket list that you haven't done yet. All that stuff."

"I'd love that, Riley. Like, I'd really, really love that."

I'm wearing a huge smile on my face as I get dropped off at my building and walk through the doors. "I think that's what this weekend did for me. When we said goodbye, I started focusing on what could be—what, hopefully, will be—and not on what should've been."

"That's a big shift in mentality," she says.

"Riley!"

A shrill voice stops me in my tracks, wiping the smile off my face.

"Shelby, what are you doing here?" I ask, as she gets up from the couch in the lobby. "I told you I didn't want to see you ever again."

"I need to talk to you, Riley. It's important. Can I please come up?"

I know girls like her. No way I'm letting her come up.

Ever.

"Shelby, as in naked-leather strap-threesome Shelby?" Ariela asks in my ear.

"Uh, hang on," I say to her, putting the phone up against my chest.

"Whatever you need to say, you can say here," I say discreetly to Shelby.

"God, you're such an ass," she hisses loudly. "I thought you might want to do this in private."

"I don't want to do anything with you, in public or in private."

"Well, you're going to have to now, Riley. Because I'm pregnant."

Read the next book in the
The Keatyn Chronicles series,
Money.

About the Author

Jillian Dodd® is a *USA Today* and Amazon Top 10 best-selling author. She writes fun binge-able romance series with characters her readers fall in love with—from the boy next door in the That Boy series to the daughter of a famous actress in The Keatyn Chronicles® to a spy who might save the world in the Spy Girl® series. Her newest series include London Prep, a prep school series about a drama filled three-week exchange, and the Sex in the City-ish chick lit series, Kitty Valentine.

Jillian is married to her college sweetheart, adores writing big fat happily ever afters, wears a lot of pink, buys way too many shoes, loves to travel, and is distracted by anything covered in glitter.

Made in the USA
Monee, IL
18 October 2022

16115391R00121